THE CURE

a novel by

Malcolm Storer

ISBN-13: 978-1530875986

ISBN-10: 1530875986

Cover design © Socciones

Design & formatting by Socciones Editoria Digitale

www.kindle-publishing-service.co.uk

Nature is pitiless; she never withdraws her flowers, her music, her fragrance, and her sunlight from before human cruelty or suffering.

Victor Hugo.

Venus was decomposing. It was as if the poison she had picked up in the gutters, from the carcases left there by the roadside, that ferment with which she had poisoned a whole people, had now risen up to ravage her face.

Emile Zola. Nana.

CHAPTER ONE

$$< M + W = J > < M - W = D >$$

Doctor Nick Slater stared at the equation. Like Einstein's $E=mc2$ it was beautiful in its simplicity. Could it be he had stumbled across a philosophical truth that had eluded mankind for centuries? As senior research chemist for Page Pharmaceuticals he'd spent the last ten years using mathematical logic to achieve scientific solutions. And now, finally, sitting at his desk in the lab, the formula had come to him. It was a simple yet elegant *<Man plus Woman equals Joy> <Man minus Woman equals Despair>*.

Is that why men acted the way they did? But discovering the truth is one thing, finding a solution something else. How could anyone possibly cure the age-old conundrum.....loneliness? And he *was* lonely. Painfully so. Why couldn't he find a partner for God's sake!? Granted he wasn't handsome – balding, painfully thin, with geeky features and the pendulous bottom lip of a village idiot – but he was loving and giving (given the chance), almost had a sense of humour and nearly always put others first. Unfortunately most of the available women in his part of Cheshire cared little for such qualities. Bagging a Premier League footballer or high octane businessman was far higher up the list. To them Nick's love of chemistry and passion for the rainforest meant nothing. He was a forty five year old unattractive bore. To be avoided at all costs. Worse than avoided; shunned.

"Here's Goldenballs."

Nick's junior colleague Ben – not bad looking himself in a boy band kind of way -- was standing at the lab window looking out over the car park. Nick rose reluctantly from his desk and joined him. Below, parking his metallic silver Porsche in the Deputy CEO parking space was Daniel Page, the boss's thirty five year old son.

Nick glanced at his watch and said the same thing he said every morning, "Late again. I don't know how he gets away with it."

Hatred of Daniel Page was the glue that held their relationship together; a constant banter proving they had little else in common. They hated his dazzling good looks, his lustrous blonde hair, his utter confidence. But most of all they hated his Svengali-like effect on women. Why did they fancy him? Nick and Ben watched in silence as he strolled across the car park in his own sweet time, joking with the security guard while miming some mesmeric move he'd pulled off on the rugby field the previous day, ending, no doubt, in the winning try.

"Look at him," said Ben. "Who does he think he is?"

Daniel knew exactly who he was. The ease in which his athletic frame filled his Paul Smith suit proclaimed that here was a man whose path through life was strewn with roses.

"I'd better get to the meeting," sighed Nick.

"What's it about?"

"Alzheimer's."

Ben puffed out both cheeks. "Whoever finds a cure for *that* can write his own cheque!"

Daniel Page strolled through a set of revolving glass doors into reception, a cylindrical whirl of sunlight announcing his arrival upon the marble floor. He was met by the good morning tones of Helen, the ravishing young receptionist. "Morning, Daniel. Good weekend?"

Walking through the lobby he picked up her musky fragrance, billions of scented molecules floating on the air like fairy dust, courtesy of Mother Nature. He followed them to the source. "Great thanks, Helen." He liked the way that, whenever he approached, she would pucker her lips ever so slightly and brush a strand of dark hair from her big Bambi eyes. She was Miss Moneypenny to his James Bond. Flirting was obligatory. "Have you done something to your hair?"

A thrilled and preening Helen leant forward, the unbuttoned V in her blouse exposing just enough cleavage (the jewels are there, if you want them.) "Yeah. D'you like it?"

"Really suits you. Yeah."

Helen watched him disappear into the lift. Flushed, she pick up the phone and pressed extension 8. "Katie! Guess what? Daniel's just come in, right, and he noticed I've had my hair done!......Yeah! Just now!"

Daniel got out at the third floor and walked towards his office along a corridor of smoked glass. To his left, the undulating Cheshire countryside; to his right, a mini industrial estate of two story buildings. Page Pharmaceuticals had come a long way since his great grandfather Joshua Page, a research chemist from Manchester, first set up the business in the eighteen nineties. Back then they supplied local chemists with tinctures and lotions. Today they were at the forefront of medical research. A far cry from Glaxo Smith Klein or Pfizer, but with Daniel soon to take over the business it was only a matter of time. He walked past the door to his father's office. He gave a cynical chuckle as he read the platinum name plate – 'Charles Page. CEO'. "Not for long, matey."

Daniel's office was next door. He entered jauntily as befits the heir to the throne. "Morning, Sue!"

His secretary was sitting at her desk busily typing. She was a matronly fifty year old his father had insisted on employing after he'd been caught having an affair with his previous secretary, a nubile twenty something brunette whose name now escaped him.

"Morning, Daniel. I've booked your car in for a service and the agenda for the meeting is on your desk."

"Cheers, Sue........And get us a coffee will you, there's a luv."

Daniel closed the door to his office just as his mobile rang. "Stevie, boy! Have I got a story to tell you! Hang on, mate, Sophie's on the other line. Hiya, Soph'. Sorry, can't make lunch today. Important meeting. See you tonight, hun'. Hi, Steve, sorry about that. Met this woman in Bubble Room last night. Great tits. Fucked her brains out back at mine. And get this, right, her husband only works for us!.........Clive, from accounts! Can you believe it! According to her they'd had a row and she was getting her own back. It's Clive I feel sorry for. Women, eh? I wouldn't trust a single one of them."

Although the headquarters of Page Pharmaceuticals was a modern chrome and glass construction, the boardroom harked back to a bygone age. The stuffy oak panelled room with its huge conference table suggested an Edwardian gentlemen's club. All that was missing was the smell of cigars and the ancient whiff of brandy. The design had been insisted on by Daniel's father Charles, a stickler for old fashioned values. He wasn't too pleased, therefore, when Daniel strolled in to the meeting fifteen minutes late.

"There you are," said Charles, a tall slim man with a distinguished mop of grey hair and the ruggedly handsome features of a retired mountaineer. "Hurry up and sit down."

The rebuke brought a smile to Nick's lips. Daniel noticed. He filed it away in his revenge folder under 'Actions Pending.' To Daniel Nick was a loathsome undercreature barely worth looking at.

There were several heads of departments sitting round the boardroom table. When Daniel finally took his seat next to Clive from accounts, Charles gave the nod to Claire Hampshire, Director of Operations. Claire got to her feet. Daniel eyed her across the sheen of lacquered walnut. Not bad. Although Claire was well into her forties, her trim figure was evidence of a well exercised gym membership. And Daniel particularly liked her heavily made up pixie face, its taut expression suggesting a demanding lover, forever craving new and challenging sensations. Nick took in the immaculate sweep of her waist accentuated by the cut of her black business suit. If only Claire would fancy him. If only anyone would fancy him!

Conscious of men's eyes scanning her body Claire blinked rapidly and cleared her throat. "Hmm-mm........This year we're sending a research team headed by Nick Slater to the Brazilian rainforest. The team will collect samples vital to our research into the areas of neuropathy-rated disorders such as Alzheimer's. We....."

"Hold on" said Daniel, blazing at his father. "Didn't you get my email?"

"Yes, Daniel, I did?"

"So you're not taking my suggestion on board then?"

"Switching our research from Alzheimer's to male pattern baldness is not an option for this company."

"But the profits from this type of research are *huge!* Baldness is massive in the States!" Daniel saw Nick smirking. "I don't know what you're grinning at, Slater! You need the cure more than anyone!" To rub it in he raised his right hand and ploughed it through his glorious blonde thatch.

"Daniel! That's enough!"

"But, Dad! All the major companies are researching Alzheimer's! You're so short sighted!"

Charles glared at his errant son. "In my office! NOW!!!"

Daniel followed his father out of the room and into his spacious office, the walls of which were hung with Hockney prints and photos of himself on golfing away-days.

"How *dare* you criticise the way I run this company!"

A nervy Daniel backtracked. "I wasn't criticising you. Honest! All I said was....."

"It's one harebrained scheme after another with you, isn't it?! Last year in was impotence, now its baldness!"

"But that's where the money is, Dad."

"Nothing wrong with this year's profits!"

"I'm thinking about the future, that's all. I mean, you're retiring soon and...."

"Hold on! Who said anything about retiring?"

Like a spoilt child denied a long awaited toy, Daniel let rip, "*You* did! Last Christmas! Remember? You said you were thinking of retiring at the end of this year and handing things over to me! You promised!!"

"For God's sake calm down! Yes, I did say I was *thinking* about retiring, but the more I look at the way you live your life the less inclined I am to do so."

"Meaning?"

"Well, *look* at you. You're, you're footloose. You live life with no thought of tomorrow."

"I see. This is all about me getting married, isn't it?"

Charles entered the Rubicon, shivering in the icy water. "Well.....yes. I want you to settle down and behave like a responsible adult."

It was Daniel's turn to wade in. "A lot of good marriage did you!" He saw his father visibly crumble. "I was out of order there, Dad. Sorry."

Charles hid his sadness behind blazing anger. "Sort yourself out! Or I'll be forced to leave this company in the hands of someone sensible enough to run it! And that's a promise!"

CHAPTER TWO

Nick parked his Volvo on the drive of his brand new four bedroom detached house. Hoping to attract a mate he'd recently sold his bachelor flat and moved to Kings Road in Wilmslow. He was surrounded by similar houses filled with happy couples with cute children who, he was certain, eyed him with Bogeyman suspicion. He stared at the empty house devoid of life. He longed for movement of some sort – a face at the window, the rustle of a curtain, a shadow encrusting the frosted glass front door -- anything that betrayed a human presence. Even a burglar fleeing empty handed would have been nice. But no. There was nothing. The house was deserted. A dead zone. Watching the film *Aliens* on TV the other night he fantasised about owning his very own android, programmed to love him and him alone. He would call her Zita, and she would fulfil his every desire, from whoring in the bedroom to Michelin star cooking in the kitchen. Come to think of it, she would look exactly like Nigella Lawson, but without the confidence. He didn't like confident women. They made him uneasy. No, Zita would take an interest in his work without yawning and would always say yes when it came to sex. And thinking about his forthcoming trip to Brazil – bearing in mind his handsome next door neighbour Steve, a hunky fireman – he could easily unplug her and store her under the stairs. But knowing his luck the house would catch fire while he was away and Steve would rescue her and she would instantly reprogramme herself to be Steve's slave.

Nick got out of his car and walked wearily up the path, glancing for a second at the unkempt lawn and overgrown flowerbed. Perhaps he could buy a male version of Zita to keep the garden tidy? No. Zita would only run off with him, along with the battery charger. He slipped his key into the lock and pushed open the door. The first few seconds were always the worst. There was no, "Hi!"

coming from the kitchen, no female feet softly padding down the stairs, synthetic or otherwise. He closed the door and traipsed into the lounge. It was furnished coldly; duck egg blue walls, pine floorboards, brown leather sofa and matching armchair, huge flat screen TV, side table and computer. There were no ornaments save for the TV remote and a large framed photograph of the Amazonian Rainforest hanging above the fireplace. He sat at his computer and logged on to DreamDates website. He entered his password eagerly ****** (Atori1). The 'IN' box flashed with a message. His heart began to race. He opened the email. There, unbelievably, was a photo of a woman in her late fifties with short dark hair and a Roman nose. She wasn't particularly attractive, but so what! Nick read the email: 'Hi, Nick. I recently joined DreamDates and read your profile. You sound like an interesting guy. My name is Sandra and I'm thirty six. I notice you live in Wilmslow. So do I! Would you like to meet for a drink sometime?'

Nick punched the air, "YES!!!" He replied instantly. 'Hi, Sandra. Would love to meet for a drink' – He thought the word 'love' was a bit forward, but decided to leave it in. Live dangerously – 'How about tonight, if you're free?'

The reply back was instant; 'OK. Great. Yeah. Let's meet at the Chilli Banana at nine!'

God! She must have been waiting by her computer, fingers poised over the keyboard. She was as desperate as he was! Hang on, thought Nick. Do I really want another desperate woman? The last one I went out with dumped me the moment she got her confidence back. But the pull was too strong. It was as if an unseen force had taken hold of him, a force so great it conquered every uncertainty and doubt. He speed-typed his obsequious reply and ran upstairs to get changed.

* * *

Driving over to Sophie's later that evening Daniel suddenly remembered he'd left his laptop at his father's. There was some hardcore porn on there he'd forgotten to erase. The last thing he wanted was his father stumbling across it! Reluctantly he turned round and drove into Alderley Edge. Passing through the exclusive village, with its trendy boutiques and wine bars, he took a left and headed up a country lane. Soon his childhood home loomed into view – The Old Rectory -- a detached double fronted Victorian villa set in two acres of mature gardens. Although he'd left home years ago the sight of the old place still haunted him. One memory in particular stuck in his mind. He was five years old, playing soldiers in his bedroom. Suddenly there was a gut wrenching cry from downstairs. He ran onto the landing to see his mother standing in the hall wearing her coat and carrying a suitcase. His father was on his knees, imploring her, "Please, darling! Please don't leave me! I beg you!" At that moment his father caught sight of him peering through the banister rail. "Think of our son. Think of him growing up without his mother!" Daniel froze. Even at such a tender age he knew what was happening. Then came the most painful moment of his life. With barely a glance she picked up her suitcase and left. He watched helplessly as his father collapsed to the floor and burst into tears. From that day on he hated his mother with a passion. Hated women full stop.

Daniel opened the front door and walked into the hall. "Hi, Dad!"

A voice came from the kitchen, "In here!"

He sauntered in and found his father hunched over the Aga removing a leg of lamb from the oven. Charles was genuinely pleased to see him. "This is a nice surprise! You'll stay for dinner?"

Glad of the warm welcome, nevertheless it irked Daniel that his father was so nice to him, especially after their bust-up in the office today. Any normal man would hold a grudge. Not Charles. Forgive and forget, that was his motto. No wonder his mother had left. Fed up of walking all over him.

"Can't, Dad. Sorry. Only came round for my laptop."

Charles held out the tray of perfectly roasted meat sizzling in its own juice. "It's your favourite."

"Honestly, I can't. I'm having dinner with Sophie in......" He glanced at his watch...... "Five minutes! Shit! I'll have to go!" It was worth it just to see the look of disappointment on his father's face. That'll teach him for smothering him with love all these years. Guilt, obviously, for his mother walking out.

"OK. Your laptop's in the lounge."

They left the kitchen and walked across the hall, scene of his father's humiliation. Daniel could picture him still, a bundle of sobs lying prostrate on the Turkish rug.

"I don't know why you don't sell this place, you know," said Daniel, glancing up at the exact banister rail where he had witnessed the terrible event thirty years ago. "It's far too big for you." Meaning, 'what the fuck are you still living here for with all those painful memories!'

"It does me," replied Charles sadly, like a male Miss Havisham.

Pathetic, thought Daniel. Absolutely pathetic! "Just a thought. Don't like to think of you rattling round on your own."

Entering the spacious lounge with its big bay windows and familiar, old fashioned furniture, Daniel stopped dead. There, on the mantelpiece, unbelievably back in place after years of being hidden away, was a photograph of his mother. Taken in happier times, she was wearing a sunhat and holding a gin and tonic, smiling into the camera. Daniel exploded, "What the fuck have you put *that* up for!? After what that bitch did to you!"

"Hey!" shouted Charles, "Watch your language! She is your mother after all!"

"Mother!? *Mother!!!!?* What kind of a mother walks out on her only son, eh?" What he *really* wanted to say was 'what kind of a spineless arsehole pines for a woman who treated him like shit!'

Distressed, Charles picked up Daniel's laptop and shoved it into his chest. "Here. Now gone on, leave. You're always dragging up the past."

"That's a laugh!! You're *living* in it!"

"That's my business! Now I'd like you to leave!!"

Business! Shit! It was always the same when he argued with his father. He would overstep the mark and then suddenly remember who was boss........who, in the final analysis, had the power to hand the business on to anyone he damned well pleased. Seconds later came the usual clawing back. "I'm... I'm sorry, Dad. I didn't mean it. It was just a shock seeing that photo again after such a long time. You're right. I shouldn't have spoken about her like that. She is my mother after all."

Daniel's mea culpa seemed to calm Charles down. "Forget it. See you tomorrow at the office."

Daniel started his Porsche and wheel-spinned up the drive, slamming the steering wheel with his fist. *"Spineless bastard!!! Spineless fucking bastard!!!!"*

* * *

Nick studied his reflection in the bathroom mirror. Stupidly he'd shaved and his skin was all red and blotchy. Too late now. I'll say I'm the outdoor type. He checked his teeth for stowaways, angling his face Picasso-like in the mirror. Which was his best side? Left or right? Probably the back of his head. Cupping his hands he took a deep breath and exhaled into them. Damn. He shouldn't have had that cheese and onion sandwich at lunchtime. He gargled with mouthwash for a third time. Anymore and he'd smell like a hospital. He put on a brand new pair of

11

jeans then took them off again – too casual. He settled for a pair of cream coloured chinos, white shirt and crimson sweater.

Luckily, as he was leaving the house, he saw his neighbour Steve pottering about in his front garden. Steve was the picture of masculinity – broad shoulders, granite thighs, with a handsome face set off by a full head of curly black hair. Nick did a mental jig. Finally he could prove to Steve he was as normal as the next bloke and absolutely no threat whatsoever to his children.

"Hi, Steve!"

"Alright, mate?"

Nick smirked, matter of fact. "Great, thanks. Off on a date.......Lady friend."

"*Really!!!!!?*" What Nick hadn't bargained for was Steve's traumatised expression, the type usually reserved for unbelievably shocking house fires.

Nick's manufactured smile collapsed like temporary scaffolding. "Yeah.....She's er........she's waiting for me."

Steve pulled himself together and manned the hoses. "Oh!....Right!....Well....give her one for me!"

Faux encouragement from a stud. How humiliating. Nick slithered into his car and drove off. When he got to the Chilli Banana his date was already there, sitting patiently at a table-for-two by the window. She'd obviously been in for a while, judging by her half empty wine glass. Or maybe she'd just bought a small one and was waiting for him to supersize. Typical! As soon as she saw him she began fiddling with her hair. Was that a good sign? It was difficult to tell with women.

Nick steeled himself and walked over. She wasn't bad looking! A lot better than her photograph. Her nose wasn't too big and she had huge breasts that swelled voluptuously inside her tight red dress. A tad past her sell-by-date but what the hell. "Hi. Sandra, isn't it?"

She got up and pecked him on the cheek. Now *that* was a good sign! "Oh! Hi! Yeah! Nice to meet you, Nick!"

They sat. Sandra gave him the once over. This was always a tricky moment for Nick. A deal breaker. He wasn't the best looking guy on the planet, and his photo on the DreamDates was flattering in the extreme. Taken a year ago in the Venezuelan rainforest, he was hacking his way through the undergrowth when a colleague snapped him in action. It was more of a joke really, but miracle of miracles, it actually made him look quite handsome in a Bear Grylls kind of way. Granted his bush hat was covering his face, revealing only the tip of his nose and a slice of chin, but that seemed to add to the mystery. And women love a mystery.

Sandra looked at him nonplussed, as though trying to decide which way this particular mystery would turn out. Nevertheless she decided to give him a chance. She had nothing else to do. She set off, stream-of consciousness, "I almost didn't make it one of my cats was ill Benny he's called he's a big ginger tom with lovely green eyes and this bloody cat from next door he's always bullying him and this time he bit him on the tail and there was a terrible shriek and Benny ran in blood pouring from his tail and I went *mad* and chased the thing off and poor Benny was in agony and this huge blister appeared and his temperature shot up but he's alright now do you like cats Nick?"

"What?" Nick felt as though he'd just walked through a hail of machine-gun fire. "Er........Would you like a drink?"

"Oh, yes please. I'll have a large glass of red.......... Do you like cats? Only it's very important."

He couldn't stand them. They were always shitting in his garden. "Oh I love cats! I love all wildlife, especially plants and trees. When I was in the rainforest last year I saw this huge......"

"Do you have a cat yourself?"

"Er, no. No, I don't." He saw Sandra's face cloud over. "I'd love to, don't get me wrong. But my job takes me away a lot so I think it's unfair. For instance, I'm going to the Brazilian rainforest in a few weeks. I'm a research chemist......"

"Is that your shop on the high street?"

"No, Sandra. Not that kind of chemist. I'm a *research* chemist. Totally different. Anyway, as I was saying, fantastic place the rainforest. Nature's pharmacy. Cure for everything in there. There's one particular plant that......."

"If you had one what would you call it?"

"What?"

"A cat, silly."

"Oh I don't know.........Tiddles, probably."

"Orrr. That's cute."

While Sandra scanned the menu Nick called the waiter over and ordered some drinks. He was desperate to change the subject. "So, what do you do for a living?"

Sandra crossed her arms and leant forward, her large breasts mushrooming inside her dress. Nick imagined unclipping her bra and burying his face in them, letting her nipples jiggle in his eye sockets. "I'm a doctor's receptionist."

Nick tore his gaze from her cleavage. "Really?.....That's interesting. Tell me more." He gritted his teeth and prepared for another volley of fire. It would be worth it, just to delve into that magnificent bosom.

"Oh I get to see all sorts me one day this bloke walked in and......."

"Bloody hell, Slater! What the fuck are you doing here!!!?"

Nick spun round. His heart sank. Daniel Page was standing right behind him, a stupid grin on his face. He wore designer jeans and a cream coloured open neck shirt, the subdued lighting giving him a movie star gleam. "Nothing! I often come here."

"Bollocks! I've never seen you!" He gestured at Sandra. "Is this your girlfriend?"

"No!" said Sandra, rather too insistently.

"Well come on, Slater, introduce me."

Seething, Nick forced a smile. "Sandra, this is Daniel Page. Daniel, this is....."

"Nice to meet you, Sand'."

Shortening her name sent shivers down her spine. She became a breathless schoolgirl again, all gooey eyed. "The pleasure's all mine, Daniel."

"He's not boring you, is he?"

"No," sounding very much like yes.

Daniel winked flirtatiously. "Just you let me know if he is. Catch you later."

Sandra didn't answer. She just stared open mouthed at his handsome face.

Daniel bent down and whispered into Nick's ear, loud enough for Sandra to hear, "Great tits. Too hot for you, matey." He gave Sandra another wink and walked off.

Mortified, Nick watched him stroll to his table on the far side of the restaurant. He turned back to Sandra, expecting her to be fuming over Daniel's sexist remark. But no. Just the opposite. She was smiling coyly. She seemed flattered. He couldn't believe it! My God! If I'd have said that she'd have slapped me across the face! Not Daniel. On no. Not Goldenballs. Women! You just can't work them out!

Sandra gulped down her wine, all the time staring over at Daniel. "*Who* was *THAT!!!!?*"

"His dad owns the company I work for. Spoilt bastard."

"Rich *and* sexy!"

Sophie was tucking into her dessert when Daniel sat down. She was a fragile thirty year old with shoulder length blonde hair, teal green eyes and pale skin, her cool Nordic features made more alluring by the plumpness of her bottom lip. She dabbed her cushiony mouth with a serviette. "Who was that guy you were talking to?"

"No one. He's a loser."

"He seemed alright."

Daniel guffawed. "He's a prick! End of. Anyway you've seen him before."

"When?"

"At the last company bash. He works for us."

"I don't remember."

"That's how forgettable he is. Anyway, I've not come here to talk about him." He slid his hand across the table, interlocking her fingers. "Listen, Sophie. I've been thinking...........We've been going out for two years now."

"Two and a half."

"Exactly.....And, well, you know how much I love you......What I'm trying to say is, I think we should get married."

Sophie's pretty face lit up, her crystalline green eyes sparkling like a sunlit fiord. "Are you....are you asking me to *marry* you?"

"Looks like it. If you'll have me?"

She flung herself across the table. "Oh, Daniel! Yes, darling! Yes! Of course I'll marry you!" She hugged him tightly, her voice full of emotion. "You've made me the happiest woman in the world!" She rooted in her bag and dug out her mobile. "I must phone Mum!"

"No! Don't do that! The company bash is in two weeks. Let's announce it then." He snapped his fingers at the waiter and ordered a bottle of champagne. "I can't wait to see the look on Dad's face when I tell him!"

* * *

Nick pushed open his front door and walked inside. Another disastrous evening. Why did he bother? Sandra had made it perfectly clear she had no intention of seeing him again. She was so enamoured with Daniel and his crass sexual innuendo the evening took a nose dive from there on in. Oh yes, she'd forgotten all about those fucking cats. It was Daniel Daniel Daniel. How old was he? Where does he live? What car does he drive? On and on! The bastard had ruined it for him. Flinging himself down on the sofa he questioned what kind of God allowed one man to have so much while others, meaning him, had so little. All he wanted was a girlfriend. Surely that wouldn't upset the balance of the universe? It made his blood boil to think that Daniel could simply click his fingers and Sandra would leap into bed! Those gorgeous breasts were ten a penny to someone like him. Where was the justice in that? Nick grabbed the remote and flicked on the TV. His favourite advert came on; the one with the sexy girl in Venice advertising cheap hotel rooms. They way she rolled around on the bed and stared alluringly into the camera melted Nick's heart. Frustrated, he quickly switched channels. Sharon Stone suddenly appeared, about to flash her private parts in *Basic Instinct.* Normally he would have been glued to the screen, waiting for the precise moment. Not tonight. He changed channels and was confronted by a naked couple having sex in the confines of an aircraft toilet. *Snakes on a Plane.* Ridiculous! He needed a safe haven; a channel guaranteed not to illicit a hard-on. He stabbed the remote and turned to the Discovery Channel. But when he saw the stunning blonde conservationist wearing a micro bikini crouched on all fours on some deserted beach helping newly hatched turtles out of their shells he threw the remote control against the wall and rushed into the kitchen. Turtles! What a waste! He opened the cupboard, hoping a comforting bowl of cereal would take his mind off things. But no. Gazing down at him from a box of Special K was a voluptuous raven haired beauty in a tight fitting red bathing suit. He slammed the cupboard door in despair. There was no escape. Sex was everywhere.

The following day Nick met his sister Jill for lunch. Whereas Nick was a balding geek like his father, Jill had taken after their mother -- a chubby, plain looking girl with a winning smile and vivacious personality. She was the type that, after a few moments in her company you forgot how ordinary she looked and was completely won over by her sunny disposition. As soon as Nick walked into the pub Jill knew something was wrong. He looked pale, worn out, stressed to high heaven. That job of his. Kill him one day. He walked over and plonked himself down.

"Well!?" asked Jill, in her usual upbeat way.

"Well what?"

"Tell me about last night!"

Nick slumped further into his chair. "It was a disaster."

"Didn't she turn up?"

"Oh she turned up alright. Problem was, first off I couldn't get a word in edgeways, then Daniel Page walked over and she started flirting with him. I don't know why I bother."

"Don't lose heart, Nick. You'll find the right woman."

"When! I tried everything last night, just like they tell you in magazines. I let her talk about herself. I listened. I smiled a lot. I talked about interesting things."

"Perhaps you're trying too hard. Just be yourself in future."

"I don't know what 'myself' *is* anymore!"

Jill paused. She noticed the rack of pain tightening across her brother's face. She had to tread carefully. "Don't take this the wrong way, Nick, but you're far too accommodating. Women like a challenge."

Nick sat bolt upright in his seat as though stunned by a cattle prod, "But I thought women *like* someone who's kind, and listens!!!"

"We do."

"WELL, THEN!!!?"

"Calm down! People are staring!"

"Yeah, and they were staring last night as well, when she pissed off and left me with the bill!" He shook his head. "It's all bullshit! Women *say* they want someone nice, but deep down they're just as shallow as men." Fuse blown, he calmed down and sank into his familiar wallow of self loathing. "And being bald doesn't help."

"How many times have I told you, women aren't bothered about that!"

"*Your* boyfriend's got a thick head of hair!"

"That's not why I go out with him!"

"No but it helps! Why can't women just be honest about what they want? Men are! Women take advantage of that."

Jill gripped her brother's hand. She stared sisterly into his eyes. "Don't become bitter, Nick, please."

"I'm beyond bitter, Siss. I'm desperate." He began to sob. "I'm.....I'm so lonely. All I want is someone to share my life with."

She got up, sat next to him and gave him a hug. "I know, I know. You mustn't give up hope, Nick."

"I tell you, Brazil can't come soon enough for me."

"When is it you go?"

"Two weeks. After the company bash......which I 'm *not* looking forward to."

"Why not?"

"Because I'll be on my own while the rest of my colleagues will be with their wives and girlfriends......as usual!"

"You never know, you might meet someone!"

Nick shook his head and stared at the floor. "More chance of meeting someone in the rainforest."

CHAPTER THREE

Sophie's mother Judy burst into the dining room. "That's it! If Daniel isn't here in five minutes we're starting without him!" She'd spent all afternoon in the kitchen cooking a three course meal and she was in no mood to compromise. "Bad manners I call it!" Point made, she turned and stormed back into the kitchen.

Sophie and her father looked at one another pensively. They were sitting at the dining table hoping to God Daniel would turn up. Both of them knew how dangerous it was to upset Judy. Chair of Wilmslow Bridge Club she was a formidable foe, destroying all who crossed her.

John, an affable, henpecked man in his sixties, gave his daughter a reassuring smile. "Don't worry about your mother, dear. Just give him a quick ring and find out where he is?"

"I *know* where he is," she said guiltily, as if the guilt was hers. "The rugby club. He's been there all afternoon. He hates it when I call him there."

"I know, Sophie. But your mother's gone to a lot of trouble."

She got up from the table. "I'll give him a ring, then." She walked into the hallway of their large detached house. Taking a deep breath she dialled Daniel's number.

"DANIEL!!" YOUR MOBILE'S RINGIN'!!!

Daniel was standing on a pint strewn table leading the packed and sweaty rugby club in a post-match singsong. Feeling a tug on his calf he looked down. Steve, his team-mate and boozing buddy, held up his mobile. Daniel could see the name 'SOPH' flashing on the screen. He thought about ignoring it, but the haze of afternoon alcohol suddenly lifted and he remembered he was he due at her house for a meal. Reluctantly he climbed down from the table; "Women!" grabbed his phone and walked outside. "Hello?"

Sophie's exasperated voice drilled into his ear. "Daniel! Where are you? You should have been here an hour ago! We're having a family meal! Remember?"

Yuck. "Sorry, Soph. Got waylaid. Go ahead and start without me."

"But we're expecting you!"

"I can't, sorry. I've got to take Stevie to the hospital! He's er, he's been injured in a tackle. He might have broken his arm."

"Can't someone else take him?! Mum's gone to a lot of trouble. She's been cooking all afternoon!"

I'm his best mate! Anyway, the rest of the lads are all pissed!"

"I hope you're not going to behave like this when we're married?"

"Bloody hell, Sophie! Don't start making demands already!" Anxious not to derail his plans – some women, even pushovers, are known to get cold feet, and he'd never find a girl as gullible as Sophie – he backtracked, telling her exactly what she wanted to hear. "Of course I won't........"The new barmaid walked outside with a crate of empties. She'd been giving him the eye all afternoon. He winked at her flirtatiously. "Trust me, Soph, I'll be the perfect husband."

The voice on the other end of the line regained its familiar warmth. "Orrr. That's nice. You go ahead and run Steve to the hospital then. I'll square things with Mum. Love you."

"Ditto." Job done, he strolled back inside the clubhouse and found Steve at the bar. A round of drinks had been lined up. Good old Stevie. Never let you down, men. Daniel nodded gratefully, tipping back a scotch then chasing it down with a beer. "Women! They think they own you."

"Some of 'em do!"

21

"Not me. Never." The singsong had subsided and the milieu was now one of comforting male drunkenness. Daniel felt at home in such surroundings, allowing him to unburden himself. "I went round to Dad's the other day. You won't believe it!" The new barmaid caught his eye; she was reaching up to get a glass off the top shelf, her breasts pushing against her T-shirt highlighting her nipples. "He's only got mum's photo on display again. Its thirty years since she walked out and he's still pining for her! I mean, what kind of a man acts like that after being kicked in the balls?"

Steve's beer fuddled brain shifted into gear. "He obviously still loves her."

Daniel slammed his fist onto the bar. "Loves her!!!? After what *she* did!!!?

"Calm down, mate."

"No one loves women more than I do, you know that. But I'm telling you, I would *never* let a woman do that to me!"

Steve had his own domestic problems simmering – recently his girlfriend had joined a salsa class and kept going on about the instructor, a handsome, pencil-hipped Brazilian who, according to her, all the women in the class fancied. He'd already given himself away once -- "Some of 'em do," -- so had no intention of joining his friend in a self pitying bout of navel gazing. Not after eight pints! "Hey, Daniel, that new barmaid's giving you the eye again."

Through half shuttered eyes Daniel saw the slim young vision leaning seductively against the optics, left hip thrust forward, head tipped coyly at an angle, the faintest of Mona Lisa smiles on her innocent face. There was something maddeningly sexy about her skinny waist – a gash of flesh between T-shirt and jeans – the way it graduated into full womanly hips and achingly curvaceous thighs. No matter how many times he'd seen such a wonderful sight – on beaches, in bars, cafes, clubs – it always produced the same effect. His mouth would dry and he would magically transport himself to some hotel room where, stark naked and drenched in sweat, he was fucking the core out of her. As usual a host of confusing signals flooded Daniel's brain -- lust, hatred, the urge to protect and destroy, to love and to defile -- all converging into the damaged junction box of his emotions. He was warrior and puppet both, with no thoughts of his own save for the thought of fucking. Tapping his fingers nonchalantly on the bar he called her over. "What time do you get off?"

"Half eleven."

Fuck me she was nice. He imagined pulling off her T-shirt and unclipping her bra, plundering her sensational tits. "Fancy going to a club?"

"Great."

* * *

After half an hour's fiddling Nick somehow managed to do up his bow tie. He preferred clip-on ones, but the man in the hire shop had persuaded him otherwise. "The ladies like a real one, sir. Shows a touch of class." And what the ladies want.....

The Page Pharmaceuticals bash was a black tie affair. Nick hated wearing a penguin suit. He could never find one that fitted him properly. This was no different. Tight where it should have been baggy and baggy where it should have been tight, he looked like a badly dressed waiter. Instead of highlighting his good points, like they do on most men, his dinner jacket was the Judas version, emphasising his badly sloping shoulders and drawing attention to his pigeon chest. What a mess. I am not looking forward to this one bit, thought Nick. Casting his mind back to the last company do, he remembered seething with jealousy over Daniel's Savile Row evening suit; the way it fitted him perfectly, the way all the girls called him James Bond and lusted after his body. Tonight, no doubt, would be more of the same. Another reason for his bad mood; not one single woman had contacted him on DreamDates, despite expanding his preferred age from mid-fifties to mid-sixties. Any older and he may as well hang around the cemetery.

He drove out of Wilmslow and headed towards Knutsford, the setting sun gilding the landscape with dabs of gold; its green fields, its barns and hedgerows, its billionaire mansions nestling behind a screen of trees. Nick loved this part of Cheshire, the exclusive village of Mere especially. He knew if he could afford to live there his lonely days would be over. He could have his pick of women then. Oh yes, they'd be queuing up to live with him then. It wasn't just the sex (it was really), although that was important. It was the companionship; hands intertwining on the sofa during a romantic movie, the intoxicating aroma of perfume in the bedroom, a whimsical smile over breakfast expressing a deep and meaningful love. It was all there, maddeningly out of reach behind those trees, in one of those very houses, just waiting for him. If *only* he could he make enough money! Winning the Nobel Prize for chemistry would do it. He imagined hacking his way through the rainforest and coming across a rare and mythical shrub whose roots contained universal healing properties. Cancer, baldness, Alzheimer's -- the holy trinity -- all would be banished from the face of the earth thanks to him. Multinational drug companies would fall over themselves. He could write his own cheque! Fame would surely follow – his face on every front cover from Reykjavik to Rio. Fame *and* money! The ultimate aphrodisiac. Women would........

"Excuse me, sir, you can't park there."

In his reverie he had parked slap bang in front of the hotel, in a space reserved for disabled drivers. The concierge stabbed his nicotine stained finger in the direction of the car park. "Over there! *There!!!*"

Arrogant fucking jobsworth! Cursing ventriloquist style Nick reversed his Volvo and parked up. Walking into the hotel he made his way to the reception desk womanned by an attractive Eastern European blonde in her late twenties with milk white skin. Small and willowy, with sapphire blue eyes, she had a delicious famished look about her.

"Good evening, sirs. Is possibles to help you?"

Yes! Please be my girlfriend. You could live with me for free. You wouldn't have to work. I'd do anything for you. Absolutely anything!!! "Er, yeah. Could you tell me what room the Page Pharmaceuticals function is in please?"

"Yes, sirs. The Cheshire Suite. First floors."

"Thanks."

Reluctantly Nick got in the lift. It had one of those full length mirrors of smoked glass that deemed to flatter. After pressing the button he took a deep breath and stared at his reflection. It was worse than expected. He looked monstrous. For some reason his head was far too big for his body – the paleness of his balding dome juxtaposed with the black tux had caused the anomaly, his sloping shoulders emphasising the point. No woman on earth could possibly find *that* attractive. He longed for the cable to snap and for the lift to plunge into the basement. Too late. Ding! The lift doors opened onto the Cheshire Suite.

* * *

Daniel was lounging on the hotel bed dressed in his dinner suit and cradling a scotch. He'd booked the room to avoid the late-night scrum for taxis. Besides, he was announcing his engagement tonight and knew he'd be pissed out of his brains by midnight. Much better to hop in the lift and fall into bed. Sophie, wearing a delicate lace bra and matching panties, was climbing into a long black evening dress. Daniel loved watching her get ready; the matter-of-fact way, post shower, she would rub scented oil all over her naked body as if it wasn't the most beautiful thing in all creation – the sculptural sweep of her hips, the peach-like globes of her bottom, her pert breasts with their raspberry nipples. And no matter how much she twisted and turned, it was flawless from any angle, as if she'd been created by a divine Michelangelo. Daniel wasn't religious in the slightest, but he figured there must be some kind of celestial architect at work to have designed such perfection. Strange how his remote sense of God was only ever triggered when gazing upon the naked female form.

Sophie put the finishing touches to her hair. "Nice of your Dad to throw a party for the staff every year."

Daniel guffawed. "Waste of money if you ask me. It'll all stop when I take over."

"Scrooge."

"Oh yeah?" Daniel reached into his pocket and pulled out a small red leather box stamped in gold leaf. He prised open the lid to reveal a platinum engagement ring topped by a massive three carat diamond, its multifaceted surface glittering amidst the folds of silk. "Scrooge eh? What do you think of that?"

Sophie was stunned. "Oh, Daniel it's.......it's gorgeous! Absolutely gorgeous!" She approached the ring like a medieval pilgrim genuflecting before the shrine of a saint. "Can I..........Can I touch it?"

"Course you can!" He removed the ring from its silken bed, the canopy of which proclaimed *Cartier*. "It's yours! Try in on!"

Hands trembling she picked up the ring, shaking her head in wonderment. It slid on to her third finger perfectly. "Oh my God, Daniel!........It......it must have cost a fortune!"

Should he? Damned right he should. "Put it this way, I didn't get much change out of thirty grand."

"Oh my God!"

"Leave it in the room until I make the announcement."

"OK. Yeah. Sure." She wasn't listening. Like Little Red Riding Hood she was lost in the ring's crystal forest.

Daniel got off the bed and slid his hands around her waist, whispering in her ear, "I want you."

"But I've just got ready."

It was typical of Daniel, wanting to spoil, to invade Arcadia and uproot its treasures. He cradled her breasts, thrilled at their firm ripeness. "Come on, baby. Just a quickie..........*Pleeeeease.*"

How could she refuse? With effortless ease she slipped both straps from her shoulders and let the dress fall to the floor. "Try not to mess my hair up."

* * *

Lost in a sea of couples Nick headed straight for the bar, bare cleavages floating in his peripheral like freshly gathered peaches. Eyes front he spotted his junior colleague Ben standing on his own in the corner. Great! I'm not the only one! Nick was about to join him when a leggy brunette wearing a tight-fitting gold dress slashed at the thighs tottered over and handed Ben a drink. Shit! He put his head down and walked to the bar. Certain colleagues acknowledged his presence. Winks, nods. Nothing too friendly; they didn't actually want him to *join* them!

Queuing at the bar he felt a friendly tap on his shoulder. "Hullo, Nick. Glad you could make it." It was Charles Page, handsome as always in black tie. Daniel was lucky to have such a well stocked gene pool to draw from. Unlike his stagnant cess pit. "Can I get you a drink?"

"Thanks very much, Mr Page. I'll have a pint of lager."

"Pint of lager please and a large scotch." While the barman got the drinks Charles leant nonchalantly against the bar as if he owned the place. Confidence. Priceless. "Looking forward to going to Brazil on Friday, Nick?"

"Certainly am, Mr Page. Cure for everything in the rainforest."

"Couldn't agree more."

"That's if the human race doesn't tear it down first."

"Quite."

Daniel and Sophie made their entrance. He left her at the door and walked over to a group of trendy young men from the IT department. "Hi, guys." He noticed Nick chatting with his father. "I see Slater's sucking up to Dad again." Helen the receptionist caught his eye. She was standing in the middle of the room with her colleague Katie. Both were wearing short, low cut dresses that showed off their tanned thighs. Daniel winked at Helen, whispering in one of the men's ears, "I wouldn't mind sucking up to her."

Did you see that?" said Helen breathlessly. "Daniel just winked at me!"

Point made, Daniel turned his gaze back to Nick. "Look at the fucking state of it! I've seen better dressed scarecrows!"

Charles left Nick and disappeared into the main room. Sophie, not really knowing anyone, wandered over. "Hi. I saw you in the Chilli Banana the other night. I'm Sophie – Daniel's fiancée."

"Fiancée? I didn't know he was engaged?"

She put her hand on his arm, leaning towards him conspiratorially. "Well, we're not. Not officially anyway. Daniel's announcing it tonight. You won't say anything, will you?"

"Course not!" It was wonderful having an attractive woman confiding in him. He could smell her delicious perfume. "You can rely on me."

"Thanks. What is it you actually do?"

"I'm senior research chemist. I look into new drugs."

"Sounds fascinating."

Bloody hell! Someone's actually interested in what I do! "Oh it is! Sadly there won't be much left to research, the way the rainforest is disappearing. I can't tell you how important it is to mankind........."

"Alright, Soph?" Daniel, noticing Sophie's cosy tête-a-tête with Nick, had left his friends and marched over.

She melted in his presence "Nick was just telling me all about the plight of the rainforest."

Daniel shook his head. "Hobby of yours is it, Nick, boring women? Come on, Soph." He took her by the hand and led her across the room. "What were you talking to that *prick* for?"

"He was on his own."

"I'm not surprised, spouting that rainforest shit! I mean, who gives a toss?"

"What about all the wildlife?"

"What about it? I couldn't give a damn if they bulldozed the whole lot tomorrow!"

Nick felt as though he'd been kicked in the stomach. Dazed, he wandered into the main room just as everyone was taking their seats for dinner. He found the right table and sat down. There were a dozen people from his department already sitting there, each with their partner. Nick made it thirteen. The ghost at the feast. He sat next to Ben, who was busy flirting with his girlfriend.

Nick felt invisible. He somehow had to materialise. "What does everyone think of the budget for next year?"

The lively chit-chat around the table ground to a halt. Who the hell's interested? We're on a night out for God's sake! The last thing we want to talk about is work!

"*I* think," said Rick, a forty year old lab technician with a huge beer gut and an obese wife to match, "that we should all get *pissed!!!!*"

Hurray! That was more like it! Nick sank further into his shell as the food was served. He caught sight of Daniel on the next table chatting amiably to Sophie's mother while Charles fussed around him filling his glass. Some guys have all the luck.

Halfway through the meal Daniel climbed onto the stage and grabbed the DJ's microphone. "Can I have your attention, please." He noticed his father staring over thinking 'what the hell is he up to now'? "Thank you. I've er, I've got an announcement to make...........Sophie and I are getting engaged."

Charles was dumbstruck. At last his son was taking life seriously. And Sophie! What a lovely girl! He couldn't have done better for himself.

Sophie's mother smothered her daughter in kisses. "Oh, darling! That's marvellous news! I'm thrilled. Thrilled!" She couldn't wait to tell fellow members of the bridge club her daughter was marrying into such an illustrious family. It would certainly put Brenda Henshaw's nose out of joint; the stuck up cow had suddenly acquired all sorts of airs and graces just because her mousey little daughter had married a doctor. A doctor for heaven's sake! The Pages could afford their own hospital!

Only Sophie's father was cagey, sipping his white wine as dark thoughts descended.

Through an avalanche of applause Daniel made his way back to his table, oblivious to a devastated Helen and a bitterly resentful Nick. Sitting down next to his father he noticed a look of melancholy etched across his face. What the fuck's wrong with him now? "Are you alright, Dad? I thought you'd be pleased?"

Charles emerged as if from a dream. "Oh I am, son. *Really* pleased." He took a sip of wine. "I was just thinking -- now don't take this the wrong way -- I was just thinking how nice it would be if your mother was here to share this moment."

That woman again! Daniel exploded, "What about *ME!!!!*?" He got up from the table and stormed into the bar.

"Goodness me!" said Judy. "What on earth was all *that* about?"

Charles stared into his napkin. "He's just upset, that's all. His mother, you know........."

Sophie's father shook his head, his premonition of dark times ahead coalescing into fact. Of course he hadn't shared these fears with Judy. After years of being told his opinion didn't matter he'd learnt to keep his mouth shut.

Sophie heard the word 'mother' and knew exactly what had caused Daniel's outburst. Countless times in bed, often when he was drunk, he would sob his heart out, hurling vile abuse at his mother. She was the queen of bitches, the very essence of feminine evil. Cancer was too good for her. Sophie realised it was best to leave him alone. Mollycoddling would only aggravate matters.

Helen noticed the kerfuffle. She got up, saying to her friend Katie, "I'm going to the bar. Do you want anything?"

"Why would I want anything? We've got waiter service!"

"I'm sick of wine. I need something stronger." She walked into the bar and saw Daniel bent over a double scotch. She approached with stealthy innocence. "Hello stranger. *You're* a dark horse."

He turned to face her. She wore her hair differently tonight. It was all curly and full of highlights. What hadn't changed was her expression -- that wolf hungry look she always gave him every time he walked through reception. If anything it was even more ferocious. "What d'you mean?"

Her low cut dress shimmered as she rubbed her knee against his thigh. "You're getting married. I'm devastated."

Daniel saw his chance. He'd often thought about asking her out but never got round to it. There were so many other girls to fuck. But now here she was, just begging for it; the way she rolled her eyes, the way the tip of her tongue slid erotically over her lower lip, moistening each delicious segment. Fuck it. From the side of his mouth he produced a cheeky half grin, his eyes gesturing upwards towards his room. "I'm not married yet, Helen." He saw her complexion flush crimson, the tell-tale sign of sexual arousal. Piece of cake.

She stared at him defiantly. "Come on, then."

Oh good. She liked it rough.

Nick was trying to start a conversation with the wife of one of his colleagues when he saw Daniel and Helen move quickly from the bar into the lobby as though hurrying to catch a train. He glanced over at Daniel's table. Sophie was talking excitedly to her mother.

"Daniel wants to get married straight away. Couldn't believe it when he asked me."

"Well, you're a lucky girl. He certainly is an Alpha male." Judy's eyes slid disparagingly towards her husband as she mouthed the words, "Unlike someone I could mention."

Sophie burst out laughing. "Oh, Mummy! You are awful!........Oh shit!"

"What's wrong, darling?"

"I've just remembered! You've not seen the ring!" She stood up. "Oh you *must* see the ring!"

"Do you mean you've brought it with you?"

"Yes! It's upstairs! Shan't be a mo."

Daniel and Helen fell into the room. Locked in a tight embrace he pushed her against the wall. They gorged on one another's mouths, tearing each other's clothes. Ripping off her bra he noticed she had bigger breasts than Sophie. He scooped them up and buried his face in them while she frantically tore off his shirt, popping the buttons on his fly. In a millisecond he was transported to the future; he could make this a regular thing every Wednesday night when he was married. He'd be sick of Sophie by then and would need to unload his sexual frustration. Helen was perfect. No, no, hang on, better make it Thursday; he had rugby training on Wednesday. Moments later they were naked. He freeze-farmed the action by grabbing a handful of hair and pulling her head back roughly. "You want it, don't you?"

Her eyes flashed widely like a silent movie star tied to the tracks. "Oh yeah. I've wanted *you* for ages."

"Oh yeah you want it all right."

She felt his erect penis rise against her bush, felt his hands all over her body as though she was made of clay and he was desperately trying to mould her. Placing his hands on her shoulder he forced her down. Helen knew the score. She peppered his body with descending kisses -- chest, stomach, pelvis – her erect nipples brushing lightly against his skin. Falling to her knees she was met by the glorious swell of his throbbing shaft. She shook her hair wildly and glanced upward, scaling the sheer cliff face of his taught body. Their eyes locked. Holding his gaze she took his penis in her hand and wanked it slowly, teasingly, sheathing and unsheathing his foreskin.

He swallowed hard, his voice like sandpaper. "Suck it."

In most areas of life he was king. Not here. Now she had the power, centuries old power as easily summoned as flicking a switch. Revelling in the feeling it gave her she opened her mouth fully and inserted the head of his cock, all the while looking deep into his eyes.

"Suck it!" he said, desperately.

She gave a big open-mouth grin and flicked out her tongue viper like. The tingling sensation drove him wild. She felt his body stiffen in anticipation. Finally she relented and sucked deep the whole length of his shaft.

"Fuck me, Helen. Fuck me that's nice!"

"Mmmmmmmmm."

"Suck it, baby. Really suck it."

Expertly she rolled her tongue around the head of his cock. He gasped, as though drenched in ice water. Sophie had never done anything like *that* bef........

"Oh my.......*GOD!!!!!!!!*"

Daniel and Helen froze. Framed in the doorway, a look of betrayal on her face, Sophie stared at the sexual tableau.

"It's not what you think!" spluttered Daniel. "She means nothing to me!"

"You bastard!" yelled Helen.

He stared down at her. The dirty slut. "This is *your* fault!"

"SHUT UP!" shouted Sophie. "JUST SHUT UP!" She took a deep breath, loading her words carefully. "I never want to see you *ever* again. Do you understand?"

Daniel felt his hard-on deflating faster than the Hindenburg. "B....but Sophie.....I...I love..." Before he had chance to finish she had vanished.

Sitting alone at the table while the rest of his colleagues gyrated on the dance floor Nick waited patiently for the outcome. He'd witnessed Daniel and Helen's flight from the room, then saw Sophie exit a few minutes later. Was it too much to ask? Wasn't it about time that spoilt bastard finally got his comeuppance? If there was God in Heaven then surely he would. But knowing Daniel he..............*Hallelujah!!!!!* A tearful and distraught Sophie entered the room and ran straight over to her mother. Nick watched gleefully as Charles, John and Judy huddled round her as she related the disgusting tale. There was an embarrassing shake of the head from Charles, an 'I thought so' grimace from John. But it was Judy who held Nick spellbound. As each salacious titbit unfolded her expression escalated from shock to boiling horror, her face contorting like a rabid Pittbull. He had never seen anyone look so angry. Without a moment's hesitation she gave Charles a piece of her mind then led Sophie and John out of the room. Nick was ecstatic. But there was more drama to come. An encore in fact. A dishevelled Daniel hurried in, shirt buttons undone, and made his breathless way over to Charles. There was a brief exchange before Charles stormed out. Daniel stood alone like a castaway marooned on his very own island of despair, his treasure ship having floated away. Devastated, he looked up and saw Nick staring at him, a curious grin on his face. Daniel bit down hard on his lower lip and ran off in search of Sophie.

* * *

Two days later Daniel was pacing the lounge of his luxury apartment wrapped in a silk dressing gown. He hadn't shaved and there was a nasty scratch on the side of his face, courtesy of Helen -- before leaving the hotel room she had flown at him, clawing, spitting and gouging. Vicious when they want to be, women. He strode up and down anxiously, dialling and redialling Sophie's house. Worryingly he had just checked her Facebook page and found she'd deleted every photo of him and changed her status to 'single'. For the first time in his life a girl had blown him out. The very thought of losing her suddenly made him realise just how much he loved her. An empty feeling yawned in the pit of his stomach. Why? Why did he go with Helen when the woman of his dreams, his fiancée, was sitting downstairs waiting for him? He had abused the only good thing in his life. Now he was paying the price. After years of laughing at his father's weakness he finally felt the old man's pain -- a pain so gut-wrenching it was impossible to bear.

Suddenly the receiver got picked up. "Hello?"

Shit! Sophie's mum! "Hi, Mrs Ross. Could I speak to........" The line went dead. He threw the his mobile against the wall. "Fucking *bitch!!!*" A wave of panic gripped him. "Think! Think!" There was only one thing for it; he would have to drive over and beg Sophie's forgiveness. He ran into the bedroom and threw on some clothes.

Slamming his Porsche into gear he screeched out of the underground car park. The traffic was light, thank God. As he took the road out of town a terrible scenario spooled through his mind. He was in his father's office and Charles was laying down the law. "You give me no choice but to leave the company in the hands of the board. I'm sorry Daniel, you've brought this on yourself." It was a double whammy -- not only would he lose Sophie but also the chance of inheriting the family business.

He turned sharp left and blasted down Sophie's tree lined road. Up ahead he saw the adorable shape of a teenage girl wearing cut-down denim shorts and a crop-top strolling along the pavement. What he did next surprised even him. Desperate to see Sophie, nevertheless he slowed down and ogled every lovely inch of her, from the tip of her long blonde hair to her beautifully proportioned toes. The usual erotic fantasy involving a hotel room sliced through his mind. He shook his head, dissolving the scenario. "What the *fuck* are you doing, man!?" He was shocked that, despite the gravity of the situation, with his future hanging in the balance, he still had it in him to look at other women and fantasise. But this was no self ordained act. It was something more profound. It was as if another person – yes, a randy Mr Hyde! – had taken control of him. He'd never really thought about it in that way before. After all, this person was as much a part of him as his heart and lungs. But this was the first time he had seen his lecherous twin in action -- glimpsed him so to speak -- and the power he possessed terrified him. He wouldn't have thought it possible. Then he remembered schoolyard tales about emaciated inmates fucking in concentration camps. He didn't believe it at the time. He did now.

Sophie's house ballooned into view; its neatly trimmed hedge and mock Tudor gables. She was in there, just waiting for him. He had to win her back. His future depended on it. Still, that teenage girl did have a gorgeous arse; the way those denim shorts slashed into her pubescent......."Get a fucking grip!!" Daniel leapt from his car and marched up the drive. He took a deep breath before pressing the doorbell.

A crab faced Judy answered the door. "What do *you* want?"

"I've come to see Sophie."

"Well she doesn't want to see you!"

"Please, Mrs Ross. I need to talk to her."

"It's always what *you* need, isn't it! Sod everyone else! Now clear off and stay away from my daughter!" She slammed the door.

Enraged, Daniel kicked it and screamed. "*Fucking bitch!!!*" He walked backwards down the drive, scanning Sophie's bedroom. He saw the left curtain twitch. "Sophie! Babes! It's me! Come down and let's sort this out! Please, I love you!"

The front door was yanked open and the dragon reappeared. "If you don't leave *right* now I'm calling the police!"

"Oh piss off you old cow!!!" Defeated, he turned and walked back to his car.

Sophie was sitting on the bed with her father – to make sure she didn't buckle Judy had sent him upstairs to guard her. She burst out crying. "Oh, Daddy. Perhaps I should talk to him."

John was all for it, but orders were orders. "Best not, darling."

The bedroom door flew open. "Did you hear what that man called me!!!? Did you!!? You're *well* rid of him!!"

* * *

"You bloody fool! You've brought this on yourself!"
Charles was standing by the fireplace while Daniel was
slumped on the sofa, head-in-hands. "A lovely girl like
Sophie and you go and do *that* to her!"

"I know. I know."

"On the night of your *engagement* for heaven's sake!"

"I know!"

"What got *into* you!!!?"

Daniel knew exactly what had 'got into him', or rather
'who' -- he'd glimpsed his other self earlier.

Things were going badly for Daniel. He'd been home
for well over an hour and still his father hadn't forgiven
him. This was serious. Really serious. He'd never known
such intransigent. Normally, after going ballistic, he
would calm down and give him the benefit of the doubt.
But something had changed. His father had the look of a
man whose worst fears had come true – his son was a
scoundrel, a rogue, a cheap lothario, and certainly not
capable of running the family business.

Once more Daniel threw himself at his mercy. "I
thought you of all people would understand, after what
happened with Mum."

Shaking uncontrollably Charles turned and screamed,
"It's completely different, you spoilt little sod!!! I never
so much as *looked* at another woman when I was with
your mother!!!"

"Pain's pain, Dad. Remember how you felt the day
Mum walked out. Never mind whose fault it was. Think
how devastated you were; the person you loved most in
the world, gone forever. That's how I feel about
Sophie.......I love her like you love Mum. I never realised
it until now. What am I going to do, Dad? What am I
going to do?"

His son's redemption plucked Charles' heartstrings. "Calm down. You'll just have to tell her how you feel. Throw yourself at her mercy."

"I....I tried, Dad. But her mother wouldn't let me see her."

"Quite right. My advice to you is, lie low for a month until she calms down."

"Good idea. I could do with a holiday."

"Holiday! We're far too busy with the Brazil trip for you to swan off!"

"Sorry, Dad. You're right......When are the team going?"

"They're flying out tomorrow."

An idea popped into his mind; one that would go a long way to reinstate his father's confidence in him. "Why don't I go with them? A trip to Brazil's just what I need! Help clear my head."

"It's no picnic in the rainforest you know."

"Come on, Dad. You're always saying you want me to take more of an interest in the research side of things. Here's my chance!"

True, he was always saying that. And getting him out of the way for a while would allow the dust to settle. "Very well. But on one condition; you don't upset Nick. He's one of the finest research chemists in the country. I don't want to lose him. So if I hear of you causing any problems, any problems whatsoever, you can kiss goodbye to your job. Understand?"

"There won't *be* any problems, Dad. I promise." He sighed. "Tell you what. I've learnt my lesson. Women are off limits from now on. I love Sophie. I'm determined to win her back."

This time he meant it.

CHAPTER FOUR

"Give me your passports," said Nick.

His two colleagues, Ben and Giles, handed them over. All three were standing in the departure terminal at Manchester Airport. Ahead of them, a long queue snaked its way towards the Air France check-in desk. Nick and Giles both let out world weary sighs that marked them out as frequent travellers. Ben on the other hand was far too excited. It was his first field trip, and the twenty year old was thrilled. He'd never been to Brazil before, and couldn't wait to see if the women were as mythically sexy as everyone made out.

"This is ridiculous!" said Giles, a fifty year old pot bellied research chemist with a grizzled black beard and large, bulbous eyes. "It's the same every time we fly Frog Airways!"

Ben smiled. Giles' nickname at work was Frog Eyes, everyone in the lab joking how at home he must feel in the rainforest.

"What are *you* laughing at?" asked Nick.

"Me? Nothing! Just looking forward to the trip."

Giles guffawed, "The optimism of youth! You'll soon get sick of it." A born pessimist, he suddenly remembered a threat issued by his wife some weeks ago – "If you don't cheer up I swear to God I'm leaving you! No one likes a misery guts!" Forcing himself to look on the bright side he cracked a smile. "Having said that, Ben, Brazil does have some fantastic football teams. I'll take you to the Maracana if you like?"

Brilliant!" exclaimed Ben. Women *and* football! It was getting better and better.

Nick cursed inwardly. He hated football. He glanced at the metal flight case containing their research equipment.

"Blimey!" said Giles. "Look who's here!"

Nick spun round. Daniel Page was strolling towards them dragging a Louis Vuitton suitcase. He wore baggy linen trousers, Armani shirt and designer shades. "What the fuck does *he* want?"

"Alright, boys?" said Daniel, fostering a roguish grin. "Don't look so pleased to see me, Slater. Dear me!"

"No, no." said Nick, desperate to hide his true feelings. "Just surprised to see you, that's all..........Going on holiday?"

Daniel looked at him deadpan. He hadn't forgotten that smartarse smirk at the company bash a few nights ago. "No, Nick........I'm coming with you."

"What!!!!"

"You heard. Arranged it with Dad last night. Thought I'd see what you lot get up to in the jungle."

The jungle! The fucking jungle! "But.....but the flight's full!"

"First Class isn't."

"But you're not a scientist!!"

Daniel wanted to grab Nick's scrawny throat and scream, 'What the *fucks* it got to do with you!' Mindful of his father's warning, he swallowed his anger and said, "Dad wants me to experience all aspects of the company......for when I take over." He noticed Nick's reaction – blind terror. He could actually see him mentally updating his CV.

Daniel added, with immense satisfaction, "See you in Rio." He winked at Ben and strolled nonchalantly towards the First Class Lounge.

Nick was seething. What the *fuck* was Charles playing at, sending that idiot along? It didn't make sense! Daniel was a pen-pusher. Totally unsuitable for a field trip! He would only cause trouble. And he was so looking forward to going back to the rainforest. *Fuck, fuck, fuck!!!!*

Half an hour into the flight Daniel was approached by a sensational stewardess carrying a bottle of complimentary champagne. She had short dark hair, brown eyes and the figure of a catwalk model.

"Would monsieur like a glass of champagne?" she purred, in her dreamy French accent.

Her beauty took his breath away. He imagined living with her in Paris; their spacious apartment a constant scene of love making. He was determined to ask her out the moment they got to Rio. Hold on! I love Sophie! I've *got* to start being faithful if I want to win her back. Come on, man! Be strong! "Champagne would be great. Thanks." This time there was no flirtatious smirk or oily compliment. He gave himself a mental pat-on-the-back.

As she bent down to pour out the bubbly, instinctively his eyes honed in on her breasts. Her uniform bulged alluringly and he could make out the lacy outline of her bra peeking through a gap in her white shirt. His expert eye told him she had conical shaped breasts, two heavenly scoops reminiscent of burgeoning ice cream cones. He imagined licking each one greedily. Horrified his thoughts were being hijacked by his 'other self', he grabbed a magazine and forced himself to stare at the front page.

"Thanks.......I wonder if you could do me a favour."

"Certainly, monsieur."

When Nick saw the sensational stewardess inching down the spiral staircase it was like watching an angel descending from heaven. There was a collective sigh amongst the male passengers in economy. *Their* stewardesses weren't like that! Get what you pay for. As she sashayed down the aisle Nick had the distinct impression she was staring right at him. The incredible thing was, she *was!*

Ben and Giles couldn't believe it when she stopped at their row, looked at Nick and asked, "Monsieur Nick Slater?"

Nick's rubbery bottom lip flapped open to reveal a line of crooked teeth. Gazing up at her he thought perhaps the plane had crashed and he was being invited to join her in Paradise – his reward from a grateful Creator for all those years of loneliness. "Y....yes, I'm Nick Slater."

"Would monsieur like to follow me?"

It *had* crashed! He must have fallen asleep and not noticed. His old Sunday school teacher was right – death wasn't painful at all! And now he was going to spend the rest of eternity with this amazing.........No, no, hang on, he couldn't have died, because when he climbed up into First Class he saw Daniel sipping champagne, and there was no way God would allow an arrogant shit like Page through the Holy Portal. Not according to his Sunday school teacher anyway.

When Daniel saw Nick walking towards him he decided to make a statement. He nonchalantly picked up the champagne bottle and refilled his glass. "The *only* way to travel. Drink?"

Nick shook his head dismissively as if such things were beneath him. "No thanks."

"Suit yourself."

"You wanted to see me?"

"Yeah. You heard about me and Sophie?"

"Well, yeah. The whole company has."

"That's one of the reasons I've come on this trip; to get away; clear my head."

"Very nice," replied Nick, sarcastically.

"Look, I don't want you to think I've come along for the ride. I intend to pull my weight."

Nick wasn't convinced. "Whatever."

"Good. That's sorted. What's the itinerary?"

"We spend the first night in Rio, catch the noon flight to Manaus, pick up our guide and head up river into the rainforest."

Daniel relaxed into his spacious First Class seat. "Piece of cake."

This annoyed Nick, especially as *his* seat was cramped and uncomfortable. "Have you ever been to the rainforest?"

"Nope."

"Well *I* have. And believe me, it's no 'piece of cake.'"

Nick's 'Big Explorer' routine didn't impress Daniel one bit. He wanted to say, "Who the fuck do you think you are, Shackleton?" But then remembered they weren't going anywhere near the South Pole. Instead he saw a chance to get under his skin. As the sensational stewardess made her rounds he noticed Nick ogling her. "Bet you'd like a piece of *that* though, wouldn't you?"

"Wouldn't any man?"

Nick's honesty shocked him, focusing into sharp relief the universal appeal of women. So, deep down Nick was just the same as him. They were brothers, bound together by an all consuming obsession – sex – just like every other shmuck on the planet. The mere thought he had anything in common with Nick Slater sickened him. He found himself saying, "Not me. My philandering days are over."

A cynical grin spread across Nick's face. "Oh yeah?"

"Yeah!" spat Daniel. "Now if you don't mind I want to get some sleep."

As Nick made his way down from First Class he past the sensational stewardess on the stairs. Close up she really was stunning. The sheer perfection of her exquisite Parisian features took his breath away – a delicate balance of innocence and seduction, earthiness and sophistication -- features that have gone on to wreak havoc down the centuries, ruining counts and cardinals, politicians and princes; vast estates down the plughole just to please the little marmosets.

* * *

The moment the aircraft door swung open they were mere puppets. That first draught of warm tropical air brought with it the promise of sex -- tiny triggers conveying subtle messages ordering them to fuck. Mother Nature couldn't really get to grips with them inside the pressurised cabin, with its litres and litres of stale recycled air and the close proximity of death. Not that she didn't have other ways to tempt them. Far from it. Glossy magazine ads featuring bikini-clad beaches and sexy nightspots kept them on the back-burner, topped up with a sudden whiff of perfume or the sight of a stewardess bending over the drinks trolley. Young Ben in particular, brimming with testosterone, had zoned in on a young stewardess with an overly made-up face. Watching her totter down the aisle he imagined making love to her inside the aircraft toilet; the white plastic light and faint odour of excrement forgotten amidst their turbulent fucking. A bomb could have gone off and he wouldn't have noticed.

They took a minibus from the airport, motoring past slum after slum. Bare-chested youths in tattered shorts hung around street corners. The light was so intense it flattened the passing shacks to a Cezanne-like perspective, a shadow-less collage of burnt reds, oranges and browns.

"Bloody hell it's hot!" moaned Daniel. He tapped the driver on the shoulder. "Put the air-conditioning on will you!"

"No air-conditioning!"

"If you think this is hot," quipped Nick. "Wait till we get to the rainforest."

None of them took any notice, not even the ones who spoke. The minibus had just entered the suburbs, and had stopped to let a group of college girls cross the street on their way to volleyball. Silence reigned inside the oven hot cab, each man mentally undressing the caravan of electric blue shorts and shocking pink vests. But it was the girl's butter smooth skin that enraptured them, its glistening toffee-apple sheen.

Nick tore his eyes away and stared at the plastic Madonna balanced on the dashboard. Giles took out a guide book, reading it upside down. Daniel closed his eyes and thought about Sophie. Only Ben carried on staring, lost in a fantasy of post-match showers and heavenly rub downs.

Looking for salvation Nick pointed to the statue of Christ perched high on Corcovado Mountain, His outstretched arms encompassing the whole city. "Look!"

"Amazing!" said Ben. He was hypnotised by this costal metropolis, its skyscrapers ringed by lush green hills, shanty towns adorning their slopes like tarnished ornaments. Now and then, through arrow straight avenues, the glittering ocean could be seen. Brought up on a diet of cheap Spanish resorts his first experience of South America blew him away. This was the real thing. Rio oozed sensuality. Hemmed in by granite mountains and expansive ocean the city was a giant Petri dish cooked by the sun. It was as if Nature had gathered together her most exotic ingredients, distilled them to their purest essence and then stood back to see what would happen. And what had happened was Copacabana.

The taxi cruised down *Rua Santa Clara,* past shops, bars and department stores. The shadowy boulevard suddenly opened out onto the sundrenched *Avenida Atlantica.* Stifled gasps were heard inside the minibus. There, in front of them, was the result of Nature's hard work -- her undeniable masterpiece -- Copacabana Beach. The men didn't stand a chance.

"Oh my God! Look at that girl!" screamed Ben, as a dark haired, loose hipped beauty wearing a dental floss bikini strolled along the tessellated sidewalk. Her body mirrored the city itself, a shimmer of subtle curves and breathtaking vistas. She was joined by three female friends, equally stunning, wearing multicoloured sarongs. One of the women had just emerged from the ocean; her hair glistening, her feet encrusted with sugary white sand. Tattooed on her ankle was a powder blue seahorse. With both hands she cupped her thick wavy hair and coiled it expertly into a ponytail, arching her back as she did so, her breasts thrust forward highlighting their firm, ample shape. The women stretched and preened, jutting out their hips languidly. The look on the men's faces said it all. You could lose yourself in this place. No doubt about it.

Ben wondered what it would be like to be a famous footballer living here, gorging himself on an endless diet of sex. Would he ever get sick of it?.........No, never. Giles compared the voluptuous quartet with his obese wife back home -- her sagging breasts, blotchy skin and acres of cellulite. What a mess. An entirely different species. Mind you, *they* didn't slouch on the sofa every night stuffing themselves with Jaffa Cakes. He'd certainly got the shitty end of the stick. Get what you pay for.

Nick was dying inside. His guts and bones ached with longing. What was the point of all this beauty if he couldn't enjoy it? What possible reason did God have for tempting him in this cruel way?

Daniel on the other hand saw things differently. As far as he was concerned Copacabana had been created solely to tempt him, to appeal to his 'other self', that devious sex addict whose insatiable appetite had brought him here in the first place. Go on, it was saying, dive in and enjoy yourself. He tried blocking out the virtuoso display of coffee coloured flesh with thoughts of Sophie. But her image kept vanishing. Defenceless, his pulse racing with desire, he vented his anger on Ben. "I thought you had a girlfriend back home!"

"I have," sniggered Ben. "No harm in looking."

What Daniel said next surprised everyone. "Make sure that's all you do."

Halfway along the *Avenida* was their destination -- the Rio Othon Palace, a 4 star beach front hotel. The minibus pulled onto the concourse and parked under the canopied entrance. A group of Swedish tourists in shorts and flip-flops emerged from the lobby, their bone white skin startling in the intense tropical sunlight. A flotilla of icebergs, they drifted across the *Avenida* towards the beach. The driver jumped from the minibus and opened the back door, dragging out the men's suitcases. Duty done he held out his hand expectantly.

Daniel, still sore about his air-conditioning quip, was quick to get his own back. "No tip!" he said, before marching into the hotel.

Nick shook his head. He dug into his pocket and gave the driver a ten *real* note (£1.50.) Now it was the driver's turn to shake his head.

The smoked glass entrance doors swished open. Trendy boutiques lined the marble paved lobby, each one staffed by a silent dark haired girl standing rigidly behind her counter. Daniel was already at reception checking in. His only thought was to get to his room and phone Sophie. He'd sent numerous simpering texts on the plane. So far *nada*.

"Right," said Daniel, heading for the lift. "See you in the bar in an hour." He got to his room and dialled Sophie's number.........

"Welcome to Orange answer phone. I'm sorry, but the person you have called is not available. Please leave your message after the tone."

"Shit!"

Beep.

"Hi, Soph......It....it's me......I just want to say that.....that I'm in Rio and.......and it's the most fabulous place on earth and........and it means absolutely nothing without you.....I love you so much......"

Daniel ended the call and collapsed onto the bed. "Oh God!" Tears streamed from his eyes. He curled into a ball, his fists clutching the sheets. Pain? He'd never felt anything like it. A soul wrenching, panic stricken emptiness washed through his body like toxic waste. How could a mere woman produce such a devastating effect? A woman he didn't give a damn about two weeks ago. What the fuck was happening to him? He buried his face in the pillow and let out a primeval scream. He'd never been on the killing floor before and found its surface cold and pitiless. He dozed off for a few hours, waking up drenched in sweat. He jumped up and tried to pull himself together. Pacing up and down the room frantically, his heart racing, extraordinary thoughts exploded in his brain. Maybe Sophie had met someone? No way! He was the best looking guy in Wilmslow! But say it wasn't about looks? What then? No, it *must* be about looks. What else was there? Money? He had plenty. Personality? Shitloads. No, Sophie couldn't have dumped him for someone else. Calmed by his rational he went out onto the balcony for some air. Darkness had fallen. Twelve floors below a necklace of streetlights traced Copacabana's gently curving beach. To his left, Sugarloaf Mountain lit by golden spotlights. To his right, the fort glimmered in the rising full moon. He could hear the waves pounding on the shore, feel the rhythm of the streets. A sultry mist had descended, haloing the streetlamps. Couples strolled hand-in-hand along *Avenida.* He leaned out and scanned the many bars bunched along the strip, their parasols like cocktail umbrellas. Directly below he saw a round shouldered figure with a bald head exit the hotel. Two other figures joined him.

BEEP! BEEP!

"Sophie!"

Daniel snatched his phone off the bed. He had a text! Yes!!!! He dived into the In Box. **Ben**. Shit!. **'Outside in bar on left.'**

Nick, Giles and Ben took a seat beneath the orange parasol, their metal chairs scraping the mosaic pavement. Nick wore jeans and a dark blue T-shirt. Giles beige coloured chinos and Manchester United football shirt. Ben, his first time in the tropics, knee length shorts and a flowery Hawaiian shirt his girlfriend had purchased off Amazon. He wasn't sure about it at first, but his girlfriend, desperate to avoid any passionate liaisons that might lead to a ten day course of antibiotics, had insisted, "You look great, babes! They're all the rage in Rio." They weren't. He looked ridiculous, and she knew it. Nevertheless, the scores of lipped glossed whores circling the bar like hyenas eyed him hungrily.

"The tree we're looking for is quite rare," said Nick. "According to Science and Nature the bark is said to have amazing ...."

"Here's Daniel," said Giles. "I'll get the beers in." He caught the waiter's eye, a dark swarthy man in his mid thirties with a pirate's smile. "Four *choppes!*"

The sight of Daniel strolling over like he owned the place got on Nick's nerves. The scruffy bastard was still wearing the same clothes! They were all creased and rumpled, like he'd slept in them. Fancy not bothering to get changed! But that didn't stop every woman in a twenty metre radius honing in on him. In fact his dishevelled appearance fascinated them. It turned them on! He'd only been in Rio a matter of hours yet already his body -- normally a solid upright chunk of muscle back home -- had morphed into that of a tropical playboy; a dreamy, laid-back lothario oozing sexuality. But what *really* got in Nick's nerves was Daniel's hair. It was stuck up in unruly tufts, as though a passionate woman had just made love to him. Nick couldn't wait to get the rainforest and hide his shame under a bush hat.

Daniel sat down at the table as the waiter brought over four ice cold beers. He seemed distant. Crestfallen. Nick wondered what he was up to. He'd expected the usual Hollywood smile and dashing confidence, not this morose, couldn't give a shit routine. Maybe he'd worked out a new strategy.

Daniel picked up his glass half heartedly. "Cheers. Here's to a successful trip." He swallowed three huge gulps, sighed, then slouched into his chair. Already his eyes were scanning the terrace for potential conquests. Whereas Nick had found only blank faces, Daniel was greeted with blossoming smiles. One smile in particular caught his attention. It belonged to a blonde teenage girl wearing canary yellow shorts and a skimpy top. She was sitting with her parents -- Germans by the sound of it. She had a cute pixie face and the bluest eyes he'd ever seen. She'd obviously been in Rio for a while, judging by her tan. The sun, eager to turbo-charge Nature's gifts, had toasted her skin a deeply alluring bronze. But the solar disk had gone further -- it had bleached her hair and swollen her lips so that she now possessed a maddeningly sexual Bardot pout. The result caused Daniel's blood to stir. A week ago he would have beckoned her up to his room and shagged the living daylights out of it. But the thought of Sophie made him turn to Ben and say, "What do you think of Rio, then?"

"Amazing! The women are out of this world."

"This isn't a holiday you know," said Nick, pissed off with the looks Ben was getting from a ravishing prostitute dressed in tight sparkly shorts and a pink latex boob-tube.

Nick waited for the inevitable backlash from Daniel. The "leave him alone you miserable bastard! He's only a kid!" But no...............

51

Daniel sat up abruptly. He grabbed a beer mat and started tapping it on the table. "Nick's right! Keep your cock in your pocket and your mind on the job!"

Nick was amazed. It gave him the opportunity to mount his hobby horse. "As I was saying.......this tree we're after is quite rare. It's not surprising really, due to the obscene amount of deforestation currently taking pla.........."

A high pitched scrape and Daniel was on his feet. "I'm going for a walk."

The table fell silent. Each man took a sip of beer and watched as the boss's son slouched off towards to beach.

Nick shook his head wearily. "I don't know why he bothered coming."

Boring fucking bastard! Daniel crossed the busy highway, dodging cars and buses. For a split second he thought about throwing himself under the wheels of a truck. What was the point of living? His girlfriend had dumped him, his father was about to, and tomorrow he faced a gruelling three week trek through that godforsaken wilderness with Slater! He strolled along the mosaic pavement with it's wave-like stripes, stepping onto the sand before stopping beneath a cluster of palm trees. He leaned against one and stared out to sea. A sky full of stars had given the ocean a florescent softness, moonlight dancing upon its surface. He felt the whole of Rio throbbing at his back. Snatches of samba and *forró* drifted on the breeze. His 'other self' emerged, filling his head with erotic images -- naked hips gyrating on a dance floor, sweat drenched breasts bunched in tinselled bras; smiles, come-ons. Trembling, Daniel took out his mobile and rang Sophie's home number. He hoped to God Judy wouldn't answer..........

"Hello?"

Sophie! It was *Sophie!!!!!* "Hi, Soph, it's m............Hello!..........Hello!"

52

She'd hung up. She'd actually hung up! It was all too much. Daniel hung his head and burst out crying. He gave way to uncontrollable sobbing, his shoulders and chest heaving violently. Tears streamed down his face, blurring his vision.

"Hey, what's wrong?"

As if through a waterfall he saw a curvaceous Carioca shimmering before him. She wore skin-tight jeans and a purple bikini top, her black wavy hair tumbling over her shoulders like an inky waterfall. She had exquisite features -- fine arched brow, aquiline nose, plump, thrust-out lips the colour of burnt cherries. But it was her eyes that riveted him -- dark pools moist with reflections from the strip; tiny sparks of neon dancing like fireflies. He thought he'd seen beauty. Not like this. Not in his whole lifetime. Nature had saved the best till last.

She took a step towards him, reached out and with her thumb glazed a tear across his cheek. Her movements were so graceful, so refined, they took his breath away. He couldn't speak. He just stared at her.

"Why?" she asked, gesturing at the tear.

At last he found his voice. "It's a long story."

She stroked his face, tracing its handsome outline. "*Belo*. Let's go for a drink."

She stepped off the sand and led him to a beachside bar she knew; a small kiosk selling beer and *sucos*. He took a seat and watched as she chatted in Portuguese with the barman -- an old black man, his face wrinkled like a prune. As she leaned further into the kiosk she arched her back, pushing out her buttocks. Daniel noticed the delicious wobble of maturity. Was there anything on earth so sublime, so perfect in its sexual symmetry. The vision drained him. He felt himself slipping away. She returned with two ice cold *Brahmas*, fizzed them open and handed him one.

"Thanks."

She dragged a white plastic chair closer to his and sat down. Lifting the beer to her lips she took a quick, birdlike sip. Smiling, she stared at him. Her smile was childlike, full of possibilities. She was beautiful beneath the palm trees, but now, drenched in the pure light of the *Avenida,* her dusky features were cast into sharp relief. He studied the contours of her face, its angelic shape; her delicate cheek bones tapering to a perfectly formed chin, the tilt of her head, the cute freckle on the upper edge of her top lip, the glossy sheen of her skin. Dear God, imagine living with her. Imagine waking up every morning next to that smile, watching her rise naked from the bed and stroll into the bathroom. What more could any man want? Why not sell up, move to Rio and shack up with her? Why the hell not? Buy an apartment and spend the rest of his days here. He could live like a king. Fuck Sophie! Fuck Dad! Fuck the business!

"How old you?" he asked.

"Nineteen."

"What's your name?"

"Luciana."

"I'm Daniel."

"Hi, Daniel." She placed a hand on his knee, her slender wrist adorned with a bangle of sea shells.

He couldn't help himself. His vision drifted from her eyes, lingered on her cherry lips, before descending into the folds of her breasts. Dusted golden by the sun they rose up to greet him.

"Pity we can't go to the Maracana tomorrow," said Giles. "There's a match on."

"Umm?" Nick was miles away. He was busy ogling a painted whore in his peripheral, a scantily clad forty something with a pneumatic cleavage. Imagine.............

"I said it's a pity we can't.............."

"I heard!" said Nick sharply, Giles' inane footy chatter gate-crashing his fantasy.

"I was talking to Ben. You hate football."

Nick glanced across at Ben. He wasn't listening either. He was busy flirting with a sublime Japanese girl on the next table with iron straight black hair and lips like crushed rose petals. She was giving him the come-on, her oriental eyes flashing wildly. What Nick wouldn't have given for such a look. All he could manage was the greedy mercantile stare of a clapped out prostitute. "Right! Let's call it a night!"

Traumatised, Ben looked at Nick. "You're joking aren't you? It's only early."

Nick pulled rank. "This isn't a holiday! I've told you! We're here to carry out serious research, not sit around all night getting pissed! We've got an early start tomorrow. I want you on the ball!"

Giles had been on the receiving end of Nick's hissy fits in the past. It was useless to argue. He looked at his watch and faked a drawn-out yawn. Tapping Ben on the knee he said, "Nick's right. Let's call it a night." He got up and drained his glass. "Must ring the wife. Don't want her to think I'm enjoying myself."

Ben took the hint. "May as well join you. I need to Facebook my girlfriend. Find out what she's been up to. Coming, Nick?"

"Er, no." That whore was staring over! Why not. Why the fuck not!! "I'll sort the bill out. On me. You go. Won't be long."

Giles and Ben strolled reluctantly back to their hotel. Out of earshot Ben seethed, "Miserable bastard! I was in there with that Japanese girl! Did you see her? Really fit she was!"

Nick watched them leave then turned his attention back to the whore; aeons past her sell-by-date but she had a fabulous body. He smiled. She smiled back.

"Where are you staying?" asked Luciana.

Daniel thumbed behind him. "The Othon Palace."

"I've never been in there. What's it like?"

"Ok...........Where do you live?"

She pointed to a mass of twinkling lights covering the hillside. "*Favela.*"

"You're not a prostitute are you?"

"No!" said Luciana, haughtily. "I go to college. My parents are good people."

"Sorry......I just thought............."

She grabbed his hand. "Take me to your room."

The ocean breeze, the balmy night, the lights, the alcohol, the transfixing beauty of this exotic bauble caused his pulse to race. He knew it was the wrong thing to do, that more than anything he loved Sophie. But his 'other self' had taken control, and it was futile to struggle. He did offer one last show of defiance. "OK. Only for one drink."

With the finesse of a skilled puppeteer she lifted him off his feet and led him across the *Avenida.*

Nick was all set to make his move on the prostitute when he saw Daniel crossing the busy highway with his arm around Luciana. So even though he'd dressed like a scruff bag and showed no interest whatsoever in women, one of the prettiest, most gorgeous examples of her sex was snuggled up close, gazing at him rapturously. Nick recalled Daniel's boast on the plane -- "My philandering days are over." Fucking hypocrite! Well two can play at that game. Nick had always vowed that no matter how bad things got, no matter how sexually frustrated he became, he would never, EVER lower himself by going with a prostitute. There was such a thing as human dignity for heaven's sake! Hadn't God given us freewill so that we could rise above the animals? Animals such as rabbits, whose every waking moment consisted of eating and fucking. Mainly fucking; the eating bit, Nick knew, only there to facilitate the sex. But surely there was more to life than sex? Wasn't there?......Nick wracked his brains, but each time he came up with an answer he shot it down in flames. Work -- something you did to earn enough money to attract the opposite sex. Hobbies -- something you did to take your mind off sex. Friendship -- something you did when you couldn't get sex. So hang on, thought Nick, that means the only reason we were put on the earth, the only reason we're here -- never mind what religion or philosophy tells us -- was to fuck. And come to think of it, wasn't everything in society -- from the cars we drive to the clothes we wear to the houses we buy to every last gadget and gizmo -- designed, manufactured and purchased for the sole purpose of procuring sex? So that was the universe in a nutshell, was it? We were no better than rabbits. Charming.

The depressing credo was strangely enlightening. It lit a fire beneath him, kick-starting his libido. If it wasn't his fault then he might as well go ahead and do it! He shot out of his chair and marched over to the prostitute, arriving just in time to see a fat American making off with her.

Daniel opened the mini bar, "Beer? Wine?"

"Beer." Luciana was exploring the room, scanning every surface with her dark, covetous eyes. She was mentally comparing the four star trappings with her dilapidated shack up on the hillside. A world away and yet so close. Often at night she would stare down from her bedroom window at the line of hotels along the strip, watching the lights flicker on and off, wishing she was a guest, married to some wealthy businessman who bought her nice things and worshipped the ground she walked on.

Daniel poured the drinks then looked at his *Breitling* watch -- a Christmas present from Sophie. They'd gone for a post lunch stroll across Wilmslow common when she'd stopped by the lake and given it to him. She looked lovely that day, pretty as a Christmas tree, her green eyes sparkling in the frost. Oh God he loved her. He loved her so much. But Luciana was inches away, stroking his arm, her eyes fixed on his crotch. She leaned forward and went to kiss him.

"Here's your drink," said Daniel, taking a step back. He took his glass out onto the balcony and steadied himself. An age old battle began to unfold. To fuck or not to fuck? To throw her out or throw her onto the bed? He was desperate to sleep with her yet he was desperate not to. He had an early start tomorrow. *So what!?* Sophie, his future, his everything, was sitting at home waiting for him. *Do me a favour!* But he loved her. *No he didn't! Think of the girls he'd shagged behind her back!* That was before he'd changed. *He'd never change! Come on! Luciana's in there right now primed and ready!*

"Daniel."

What are you waiting for?

Daniel stepped back into the room. "I think you should leav........" Luciana was lying naked on the bed, her voluptuous body draped across the sheets, her long black hair cascading over her breasts. The silken masterpiece opened her arms, beckoning him forward. He tried, he really tried to resist, to throw her clothes at her and ask her to leave. But that was never going to happen. Kings had fought wars over women like this. Lost their crowns and their kingdoms. Strong men with backbones of steel. What chance did he have? She raised her head off the pillow, fixed him with a stare and inched open her legs, grinning at her own salaciousness. Snakelike her arm swam down her body, her fingers teasing apart the coral pink lips of her vagina. The power she possessed thrilled her. Strange, his feet were moving of their own accord. They were moving forward, not back. Towards the bed not away from it, like his brain wanted them to. What the hell was going on? In a bravura display of supreme manipulation the Divine Electrician had rerouted nerve endings, jammed junction boxes and bypassed neural circuitry, isolating his moral compass. He threw off his clothes -- shirt, trousers, underwear -- while the naked nineteen year old readied herself, cupping her breasts and massaging them roughly, opening her mouth and tonguing her nipples. God help us. He dived onto the bed and into the fleshpot, ransacking her body.

CHAPTER FIVE

The mood on the flight out of Rio was tense. Some idiot had seated Daniel and Nick next to each other. So while Giles and Ben chatted in the row opposite, Daniel stared out of the window, desperate to avoid conversation. The view wasn't to his liking -- for the past three hours all there was too see was an endless carpet of rainforest, mile after mile of it. The plane wasn't to his liking either; zero legroom, terrible food, and a distinct smell of rotten meat emanating from the galley. He kept glancing at Nick, hoping he was as uncomfortable as he was. But no. Stoic Slater seemed quite happy reading his Greenpeace magazine.

Both men had sex on their minds, but for different reasons. Each silently poured over last night's events. Daniel was ashamed of himself, frustrated he'd let himself down by sleeping with Luciana. Nick was ashamed of himself, frustrated he'd let himself down by not sleeping with the prostitute.

"Any rubbish?" asked the stewardess, holding out a black bin bag.

"This airline!" spat Daniel.

Nick chuckled inwardly. Just wait till we get to the rainforest -- the heat, the flies, the hardships. The prospect of watching Goldenballs struggle through every energy sapping, insect ridden day delighted him. He smirked, a little too blatantly. Daniel noticed. For the past fifteen minutes Nick had been tut-tutting his way through an in-depth article about the impact of deforestation on the Amazon Basin. It got on Daniel's nerves the way that, as he got to the end of each page, he shook his head, licked his finger and flicked over to the next one noisily.

Desperate to get his own back Daniel gazed out of the window at the expanse of greenery stretching from horizon to horizon. There seemed no end to it. "I don't know what all the fuss is about?"

"Sorry?" said Nick, shocked that Daniel had finally spoken to him.

Daniel pointed out of the window, stabbing his finger at the ground. "The rainforest. There's loads of it."

How childish, thought Nick, well aware Daniel was trying to goad him. "Good night last night?"

Daniel smelt a rat. "Not bad, you know......."

"Only I thought your philandering days were over."

"Meaning?"

"Just that I saw you going into the hotel with a girl on your arm."

Shit! thought Daniel. If he tells Dad I've been shagging around I'm finished! "Oh, her!..... She er......she was lost......I er......I took her to reception."

Nick grinned as if to say, 'Oh yeah?'

Daniel had the weirdest feeling Nick could see right through him. That the proud boast he'd made on the flight over to Rio was nothing but bullshit, which it was, proving he didn't have one ounce of self control, which he didn't. The realisation angered him, festering a boiling hatred for the bald inquisitor.

"Ladies and gentlemen, we will shortly be landing in Manaus."

As Nick went to grab his seatbelt and tightened the strap, Daniel stared at him menacingly. "That's right, buckle up. We're in for a bumpy ride."

* * *

The six seater Land Rover careered down the rutted track, pitching and rolling like a storm tossed boat.

"How much further?" asked Daniel impatiently. He was sitting in the back with Ben, pissed off with the heat and humidity, the endless jungle scenery, already regretting his decision to come on the trip.

Above the din of the engine a doom laden voice sounded from the seat in front. "Another four hours at least." Nick glanced at Giles as he said this, a suppressed grin cracking his face. Beyond Giles was the driver, a swarthy mulatto in his late forties wearing a red check shirt, cowboy boots and ripped jeans, a cigarette wedged between his lips.

"Four hours! Fuck me! We've been travelling for six already!" Daniel held on tight as the Land Rover hit yet another pothole, throwing him against the side of the cab. Ben delved into his bag and offered Daniel a bottle of water. He refused, then changed his mind when Ben went to put it back.

After landing in Manaus they had jumped in a taxi and headed across town to a one storey office surrounded by a concrete yard ringed with razor wire. Ortega Tours had been operating since the mid 90's, hiring vehicles, drivers and guides to the many pharmaceutical companies keen on plundering the Amazon. Nick had used Ortega before. He liked the fact that their driver-come-guide, Pacon, was part Amazonian Indian and knew each of the tribes living in the rainforest. Despite looking like a cut-throat, his extensive knowledge and fluent language skills had smoothed the path of many a successful field trip.

Nick adjusted his bush hat. "Tell me, Pacon. Any sign of illegal loggers where we're going?" He saw Daniel roll his eyes in the rear view mirror.

"They are like bandits, sir. They strike here and there, a law unto themselves, and make off with Nature's bounty."

"Terrible."

"Yes, sir. Soon there will be no plants left to collect."

The orange dirt road continued, mile after twisting mile, sometimes shaded by massive overhanging trees, sometimes opening out onto areas of deforested scrub. Each time they came upon these scorched landscapes Nick would bemoan Man's cruelty towards the planet. Daniel was too busy thinking about Sophie to be bothered about the planet. What was she doing? And who was she doing it with? The vast continent separating them was too much to bare. He wondered how his spray of two dozen red roses had gone down, ordered earlier this morning via the desk clerk at the Othon Palace. "Any message, sir?"

"Yes," said Daniel, watching Luciana's superb arse jiggle out of the lobby. "To my darling Sophie. I love you so much. Daniel."

The clerk, having witnessed Luciana's tearful farewell and Daniel's touching promises to return, gave him a man-of-the world grin. These *gringos!*

Towards late afternoon they came to a small riverside village. The residents were dirt poor fishermen, part Indian, part Brazilian, who lived with their families in corrugated shacks by the waterside. Rickety wooden jetties ran from each of the shacks and stretched part way into the river. Close to the bank old men sat mending nets while naked children buzzed around like mosquitoes. Outside the numerous dwellings women chatted or hung out the washing. As soon as the Land Rover appeared the children ran towards it screaming wildly.

"Here we go!" laughed Giles. He jumped out and produced a packet of sweets, handing them out gleefully.

Daniel opened the door and straight away noticed the smell, a putrid mix of rotten fish, dank mud and dog shit. "What a dump!" He was all for 'going native' -- one time he and Sophie had slummed it in the Maldives visiting a local market -- but this was ridiculous! While Nick chatted to the Pacon, he and Ben got out of the Land Rover and stretched their legs.

"This place is right out of National Geographic," said Ben, gazing hypnotically at the slowly winding river disappearing into the jungle.

"I'd cancel my subscription if I were you!" quipped Daniel. His backside was numb and already he'd been bitten on the neck by a mosquito. "Who in their right mind would want to live here!"

Ben pointed at the river. "Is that the Amazon?"

"How the fuck should I know! Probably."

"Awesome!"

"Don't start, Ben!"

"What d'you mean?"

"With this rainforest shit. Slater's bad enough!" He picked up a tin can and threw it into the river. "I wonder what our hotel's like?"

Ben's face clouded over.

"Is it a shit hole?"

Ben stammered, "Didn't Nick tell you?......We're...we're staying with the driver and his family."

"Pacon! Does he own a hotel?"

"Not really."

"Well where are we staying then?"

Ben gestured over Daniel's shoulder. Daniel turned to see Pacon leading Nick inside a two storey hovel cobbled together from planks of wood and grimy sheets of tarpaulin. Outside the front door scrawny chickens pecked in the dirt. "I am *not* staying there!"

"There's nowhere else to stay."

"There *must* be!" Daniel saw Nick exit the shack. "Right!" Fuming, he marched across the clearing. "Nick! Nick! What the *fuck's* going on!"

"What are you talking about?" His mobile rang. "Hello?.......Oh hello, Mr Page......."

Daniel froze.

"................Yes, Mr Page, we've arrived safely. Thanks for your concern. Yes, yes, everything's fine. We're spending the night here then the guide's taking us up river at dawn..........Daniel? He's.............."

Daniel snatched the phone. "Hi, Dad! Great to hear from you. How's things? Me? Fine, fine. It's a fantastic place. Really glad I came. Can't wait to get into the rainforest tomorrow." He lowered his voice, slinking off behind the Land Rover. "Has Sophie been in touch by any chance?.......No.......Ok, not to worry. Speak to you soon, Dad. Bye." Sick to the stomach he slumped against the door. Despite sending her flowers she still hadn't responded. Perhaps she'd dumped him after all. This was serious. Really serious. The heat suddenly hit him. His vision began to blur, the mud brown shacks melting like wax.

"Did you want me?"

Daniel wiped the sweat from his eyes. "What?" Nick was standing next to him, pulling his rucksack from the rear of the Land Rover. "Oh yeah. Ben said we were travelling up river tonight."

"Tonight! What's he talking about!" Annoyed, Nick motioned Ben over.

"Don't bollock him. He's probably got mixed up. We're not all on the ball like you."

"Yeah?" asked Ben.

Before Nick could speak Daniel jumped in, "Don't stand around with your finger up your arse. Grab the rucksacks and take them inside." He turned to Nick. "I believe we're staying at chez Pacon. Lead the way."

They trudged across the clearing to Pacon's hovel, entering through a tatty curtain hung up to stop the flies. Sparsely furnished, with a rickety wooden table and four raffia chairs, the house was spotlessly clean. There was a sink, a tiny calor gas stove and a bamboo dresser containing cracked earthenware plates. Above the sink was a row of pots and pans. The roughly decorated walls were hung with peeling yellow wallpaper. Pride of place was a kind of shrine containing plaster saints. A single kerosene lamp hung mournfully from the ceiling. Daniel shuddered.

"Nice of you to put us up, Pacon," said Nick.

Pacon was sitting at the table pouring out a glass of *pinga,* while his wife, a thin, dusky woman in her forties, stood peeling potatoes at the sink. "It is nothing. My children are sleeping elsewhere tonight. You can use their room." He pointed to a set of wooden stairs. "Up there on the right. Join me for a drink once you've settle in."

Ben entered carrying the rucksacks. The three men climbed the narrow staircase, the whole shack swaying from side to side. It reminded Daniel of a tree house his father had built for him not long after his mother walked out. He soon got bored with it, and burnt it down one night for a laugh, blaming it on council estate thugs. The room they were staying in was tiny and reeked of poverty. It was more like an artist's garret, with bare sloping floorboards and a crude skylight. Two mattresses stuffed with straw lay in each corner propped up on pallets. His and hers, judging by the football poster over one and a photo of a kitten torn from a magazine over the other.

"I'm not sleeping in here!" said Daniel.

Nick was mortified. *"Shusssssh!!!!* Pacon will hear you!"

"I don't give a shit. I am not dossing down with you three farting all night." He grabbed his Louis Vuitton rucksack off Ben. "I'm sleeping in the Land Rover!" He trundled downstairs noisily, sending shock waves through the paper thin dwelling. "Thanks for the offer of the room, Pacon. Unfortunately I've drawn the short straw and the guys have banished me to the Land Rover." He pulled back the ragged curtain. "Back in a mo. Hold that drink."

Fifteen minutes later they were sitting round the table knocking back sugarcane rum. Night had fallen, the glow from the kerosene lamp casting eerie shadows on the wall. The light formed a kind of halo, the far corners of the shack receding into darkness. Now and then Pacon's wife could be glimpsed, ghostlike in the blush of a single candle as she prepared the evening meal. Pacon regaled them with macabre tales from the rainforest -- the time when a German scientist went missing, never to be seen again; the day he was ambushed by a tribe of head hunters, narrowly escaping with his life. He'd once seen a giant Anaconda eat a full grown deer! Ants the size of rats, rats the size of cats. It was true! All of it! *"Saúde!"* Pacon tipped back his drink and slammed his glass down onto the table. Daniel did the same. "Cheers!" followed by Ben and Giles. Nick politely declined, putting his glass down gently before glancing at Pacon's wife for approval. Another round of drinks were sloshed into glasses.

"I once saw a giant lizard at Chester Zoo," said Ben.

Everyone burst out laughing. Daniel felt at home in the all male milieu. It reminded him of Wilmslow Rugby Club. You can't beat male company. No women to spoil things. As he glanced round the shack he felt envious of Pacon. He didn't have much, but at least he was master in his own home -- getting steadily drunk with his *compardres*, his dutiful wife preparing the evening meal -- unlike his father Charles, whose spineless behaviour created a monster. He imagined Pacon putting up with his mother's constant mood swings. I *don't* think! One kick from those cowboy boots and she'd soon know who's boss. And what if he did have affairs with other women -- Pacon looked the type -- the mouse in the corner certainly wouldn't say anything. She'd more than likely be proud. Proud that he'd chosen her above all others to cook and clean. Yes, these so called backward people could teach Western men a thing or two about women. Daniel laid the blame firmly at the door of Cosmopolitan, that shallow magazine whose half baked articles in the 80's encouraged men to get in touch with their 'feminine side'. And like lemmings the men complied, sitting around discussing their 'feelings'. Half a million years of dominance down the drain. And for what? An 'insight' into the female mind! God knows what the Romans would have made of it. No wonder there was an upsurge in lesbians. They were the only real men these days. They had balls, and weren't afraid to use them.

One impatient glance from Pacon and the meal was delivered piping hot to the table -- fried chicken with rice and black beans. The mouse scurried back to her corner.

No sign of Cosmopolitan in this house. They dined like kings. Daniel particularly admired Pacon's revolting table manners -- talking with his mouth full, sucking the life out of every chicken bone before lobbing it into the sink with a clank. "Bingo!" He'd obviously had a lot practice. His son might sleep on a mattress, but what an example he was being set! After the meal Pacon suggested going to the local bar. By now the alcohol had infused the men with macho indifference. Giles, who wouldn't have dared go to the pub after his wife had cooked a meal, threw back his drink, burped like a pig and said, "Count me in!"

Ben, normally a pushover when it came to women, was seized by a misogamist desire to rub the mouse's nose in it. He gave her a cursory glance, slammed his glass onto the table and exclaimed, "Boys night out! Bring it on!"

Daniel was witnessing something magical. It was like going back to those great medieval banqueting halls where men ruled the roost and women were shagged and not heard. Only Nick let the side down. He leaped out of his chair and began collecting the plates and glasses. "You go. I'll help Pacon's wife with the washing up."

Pacon had never seen anything like it. He looked at Daniel and shrugged his shoulders as if to say, 'Is this how the English now behave? They who had once conquered the globe! Pathetic!'

They all piled out. A night-time choir of cicadas surrounded them, underscored by a chorus of bullfrogs. They followed Pacon up a dirt road lined with slanting hovels and jerry-built shacks. Snatches of conversation could be heard; shouts, laughter, the distorted voice of a football commenter. Suddenly a ragged curtain was pulled back. In the blazing doorway a teenage girl breastfed her baby. Inside the shack a semi-naked man sat reading a newspaper. The curtain fell. All was starlight.

"You'll like this place," said Pacon. "The barmaid!" He kissed the tips of his fingers.

Daniel grinned. Pacon was his hero. He imagined growing up under such magnificent tutelage. At school, for instance, on parent's evening, when the headmistress showed Pacon the sorry state of affairs that was Daniel's report book -- instead of grovelling and promising to send his son for extra lessons, like Charles had done -- Pacon would have told her to go fuck herself. *His* son had no need of an 'education'. There was a big wide world out there waiting with its legs open. As for Page Pharmaceuticals, with Pacon at the helm all sorts of quack remedies would be peddled -- sensational cancer treatments, revolutionary dementia cures, not forgetting the holy grail, baldness -- with a huge and profitable sideline in Class A drugs.

Zico's was a tin-roofed drinking shack located half way along the wharf; a place where local fishermen came to play pool and drown their sorrows. A single red light cast a hellish glow above worm eaten bar stools and upturned packing cases standing in for tables. Flies circled noisily in the stifling air, the stench of fish overwhelming. Not that the men noticed. The moment they walked in they were captivated by the barmaid. Away from prying eyes Mother Nature had been busy with her experiments. Spurred on by logger's lust and the naked innocence of the natives, she'd had the audacity to mix Indian blood with that of the incomer. The result, a jaw dropping twenty year old of such incomprehensible beauty the only sensible thing to do was to bow down and worship her. Daniel thought Luciana was sexy. This girl blew her out of the water. The men were speechless. Ben felt like shooting himself. Giles realised his existence had been meaningless up to this point. And she was only the prototype! A few tweaks here and there down the generations and Mother Nature would have reached her apotheosis. Forget global warming, terrorism or famine; once these weapons of mass seduction found their way out of the jungle and were unleashed upon mankind it was only a matter of time before Armageddon. Men would kill for a mere glimpse of them. Billionaires would squirrel them away, leaving them their entire fortunes. It wouldn't be long before they were voted into office, ruling the world in sexy sisterhood. Soon every diamond mine on the planet would be exhausted -- alligators hunted to extinction for their skins; jaguar, cheetah, sable and mink for their pelts -- every precious resource plundered in order to satisfy these fantastical creatures. And finally, after an orgy of consumerism, the world would destroy itself in one gigantic fuck fest.

Pacon chuckled at the men's reactions. He led them to a table in the corner. All three sat with their backs to the bar in stone cold silence. They had witnessed something so wonderful, so utterly mesmerising, they had ceased to function. Terrified of looking round even, it was left to Pacon to fetch the drinks.

"Here," said Daniel, handing him a 1000 Real note.

"But, sir! This is too much!"

"No, no. Tell her to keep the change."

It had begun.

They were so drunk when they left the bar their final glimpse of her was nothing but a blurred and indistinct glaze of colour. It was only when they tasted fresh air that the memory of her beauty coalesced.

Giles......"Did you see........"

Ben........"Oh my God........."

Daniel....."Unbelievable....."

"What did I tell you," said Pacon ruefully, his debauched features glistening with sweat. "A real gem."

They staggered back to Pacon's shack. Daniel climbed into the Land Rover and collapsed across the back seat. Just as he was falling asleep a terrible din made him sit up. Through the window he saw Pacon cowering outside his dilapidated duplex while his wife went to work on him, shouting and screaming obscenities, raining down blow after blow with her skillet...............So, the mouse ruled the roost then.

CHAPTER SIX

It was a chastened and morose Pacon that tapped on the window and wrenched Daniel from his rum fuelled slumber. Lying on the back seat, dead to the world, he had a splitting headache. He took a deep breath, rubbed his eyes and sat up. "Oh God." Someone had poured powdered glass into his mouth.

"Morning, sir. Breakfast is ready."

Daniel creaked open the door. "What time is it?"

"Dawn."

In the roseate glow he saw a group of fishermen climbing into their boats. A blanket of mist hung over the river, shrouding the far bank. Hideous monkey chants pierced the morning silence. Daniel winced. "What the hell's that?"

"The children of the forest."

"No!" He pointed to a massive bruise on the side of Pacon's face. "That!" Then he remembered last night's domestic bust up. "Oh, shit. Sorry."

"Ah, you saw did you, sir?"

"Fraid so."

Pacon hung his head and came over all philosophical, "Women. Such strange creatures. So hard to predict, no?"

Daniel slid out of the Land Rover. "Sure are. You mentioned something about breakfast? I'm starving!"

"Follow me. Your colleagues are already eating." They walked across the clearing. As they neared the door to his shack Pacon tugged Daniel's sleeve. "If you don't mind, sir, I would appreciate it if you didn't speak about what you saw last night.......I er, I told your colleagues I had fallen down the stairs."

"Fine by me."

"Thank you, sir."

Daniel pulled back the curtain to find Nick, Ben and Giles tucking into slices of melon, smoked meat and buttered bread, a pot of steaming coffee percolating on the stove. He took his seat at the table. "I feel like shit."

"Me too," moaned Ben.

Giles chimed in. "What the hell were we drinking?"

Rinsed clean after a blissful night's sleep Nick decided it was time to focus on the day ahead. "Now, the tribe we're staying with are called the Atori. Their knowledge goes back centuries. They know every flower, root and herb in the rain..........."

Daniel's heart sank to his boots. In the corner of the shack he saw Pacon sidle up to his wife, kiss her on the cheek and whisper poetic phrases in her ear. The mouse pushed him away, but he persisted, stroking her face gently, pleading with his bloodshot eyes. More humiliation -- she picked up the dishcloth, shoved it into his midriff and glared at the sink. The only thing preventing Daniel from thinking about Sophie was Pacon's shining example of manhood. Here at last was someone worthy of his respect, someone he could look up to, whose cocksure machismo blazed like a comet. But now the scales fell from his eyes as he witnessed Pacon, shoulders slumped, standing at the sink scrubbing the very skillet his wife had battered him with. Seems he was just like every other guy on the planet when it came to women -- a weak, spineless wimp. His defences crumbled. Freed from her mental prison Sophie's face loomed into his mind, all the more beautiful for its absence.

Ben gave him a nudge. "Try this melon, it's.........."

"I'm not hungry."

After breakfast they grabbed their rucksacks and gathered at the edge of the wharf. For some reason Daniel expected to see a motorboat tied up fuelled and ready. He was shocked when Pacon handed each of them an oar and told them to get into a six man canoe. Pacon sat in the back and held the craft steady while they clambered aboard.

"OK," said Pacon, offering them his bruised profile. "The Atori village is around five kilometres downstream. I'll steer. And please, listen to what I say at all times."

They pushed off from the bank and paddled to the dead centre of the river where the current was at its strongest. Soon they were out of sight of the village, drifting gently into the interior. As the sun rose higher, illuminating the forest, so the colours intensified. Crumbling orange sandbanks exposed pink and yellow flowers, the shadowy foliage deepening to a blue-green hue, impenetrable and awe inspiring. Now and then a gentle breeze brought intoxicating fragrances drifting across the river, making the men light headed. Floating along the glass smooth surface Nick was humbled by the sheer profusion of life. Truly this was Nature's laboratory; a holy place, where the fundamental elements of life, forged within stars and scattered throughout the cosmos, were mixed and blended.

"Look at the size of that rat!" exclaimed Ben, pointing at a huge brown rodent with enormous teeth scurrying along the bank. "You were right, Pacon!"

Pacon shook his head. "Capybara."

"Hydrochoerus hydrochaeris," added Nick, showing off. "It's a kind of giant guinea pig. Very tasty."

"You must be joking!" said Daniel.

"You'll find out soon enough. It's a specialty of the Atori."

"What!!!"

The further they paddled the more insignificant they became. To the gigantic trees they were merely ants floating on a leaf. Primeval sounds reached their ears -- terrible squawks and spine tingling roars.

"We are getting close to the Atori village," said Pacon.

74

Fear of the unknown gripped Daniel, a morbid, deep rooted fear that dried his mouth and gnawed at his guts. Half hour later they rounded a bend in the river and breached the canoe onto a shallow sandy beach. To everyone's amazement Pacon cupped both hands to his mouth and let out a high pitched bird call. Moments later two semi naked Indians emerged from the forest carrying machetes. The men were short in stature and wore beaded bandanas spiked with porcupine quills, a garland of shells decorating wrists and ankles. Their faces were tattooed in dark blue ink applied in concentric circles. Both had glistening, domed shaped hair.

"Look at the state of this lot!" said Daniel, warily.

Pacon climbed out of the canoe and walked up the beach to greet them. They shook hands warmly. The men grinned, displaying a row of sharpened teeth. They spoke in *Arawak*, an ancient language that produced in Daniel vivid pictures of blow pipes and shrunken heads.

"Right. Let's get this show on the road," said Nick.

The men got out of the canoe. Ben unloaded the rucksacks, placing them on the sand. Daniel couldn't take his eyes off the Indians; he'd only ever seen such colourful characters on TV. They seemed friendly enough, but that was just a ruse. He knew the moment his back was turned those machetes would be put to good use. Pacon gestured to the men to come forward. Daniel hung back as Nick strolled forward, shaking hands with the Indians. Ben and Giles did likewise, eventually followed by Daniel.

"Distant cousins of mine," said Pacon. "Trumac and Rapau. Trumac is the Atori chief."

Nick nodded. "Ah yes. I've met Trumac before."

Rapau looked at Nick curiously, scrutinising his face. He'd seen something similar atop a totem pole.

"Everything is arranged," said Pacon.

Trumac beckoned everyone to follow. They headed off into the rainforest. Instantly the sky was blotted out by massive trees draped in jungle creepers. Trudging single file along a narrow pathway the air was redolent with the heady scent of fruits and flowers. The tortured call of a howler monkey boomed through the forest. Strange looking mammals crept along moss covered braches. Shafts of sunlight sliced through the canopy, spotlighting swarms of ants carrying off a bird eating spider. Daniel felt hemmed in. The air was moist and clammy. But far worse was the soundtrack to this steamy cauldron, a kind of high pitched static that plagued the ears like a distorted radio.

After an hour's trek they came to a clearing dominated by a huge oval shaped structure thatched with palm leaves known in *Arawak* as a *Tabanau*. Gangs of near naked women adorned with animal teeth and brightly coloured feathers came rushing to greet them. They were invited into the *Tabanau* and seated under the eaves. Partially roofed, the centre was open to the elements. A strong odour of Ancient Man hung in the air -- an earthy combination of musk, sweat and dung. Nick, Daniel, Giles and Ben, who were sitting in a line, suddenly became aware of these long lost essences. They triggered brief flashes of subliminal memory, feelings rather than images, a powerful and overwhelming sense of déjà vous. Bewildered, the men looked about them, sniffing the air. Trumac issued orders to the various members of the tribe who nodded and went about their duties. From beneath his bush hat Nick's eyes lingered on the receding cheeks of an Atori girl's bottom, the samba-like sway of her hips.

Pacon announced, "The chief has ordered the tribe to prepare a ceremonial meal of welcome. It is a great honour he is bestowing on you."

"Oh! Tell the chief thank you very much!" said Nick, effusively. "Hear that guys!"

All the men nodded.

Daniel whispered in Ben's ear, "Let's hope giant rat's not on the menu." Ben sniggered. As he said this Daniel noticed Trumac studying him with a look that said, 'We might be a primitive people, but we know when a scorpion is amongst us.' Daniel panicked. Clasping his hands together in supplication he leant forward submissively and said to Pacon, "Please tell the chief we are unworthy of such a magnificent gesture," nodding obsequiously and smiling at Trumac. "And tell him it is *we* who are truly honoured."

Nick couldn't believe what he was hearing. Nothing Daniel said had come from the 21st Century. Pacon relayed the message. The chief deigned a thin lipped smile, his eyes narrowing distastefully as he took in the full extent of this odious creature.

Daniel was relieved when Nick got to his feet and said, "OK, guys, let's check the gear."

Late in the afternoon a hunting party returned carrying a small dear, two monkeys and a wild boar. Trumac told the women to gather plantains and yams from their cultivated plots. At dusk the carcasses were skinned and butchered, the entrails thrown to the dogs. Beneath a blood red sky flecked with orange and gold Daniel watched as the animals tore into the offal, frantically gulping down unchewed mouthfuls of steaming liver and lungs. Trumac ordered the hunters to build a huge bonfire in the centre of the *Tabanau.* When it was lit, great tongues of flame shot up into the sky. Raffia mats were rolled out and the tribe gathered at the fire's edge, the crackling glow illuminating their Neolithic faces. Pacon beckoned the men over. As honoured guests they were placed next to Trumac, who was sitting cross legged in the centre. An excited chatter rose up as the food was served on glistening palm leaves.

"It is rare for the tribe to eat meat," explained Pacon.

The guests were offered the choicest cuts, barbecued and laced with spices, brought to them by teenage girls. A sensual thrill ran down the men's spines. Nick zoned in on one girl in particular. She was around sixteen years old, with bronze arms, sleek hips and heavy breasts. He imagined taking her for his wife, joining the Atori and living out his life in jungle splendour. He would liquidate his assets and set up an account in Manaus. A million pounds would go a long way in a place like this. These people had nothing. Imagine how grateful they would be! The women especially!! It wouldn't be long before he had his own personal harem. But he wouldn't spoil them, oh no. He'd seen what had happened to the pampered women of Cheshire. Steeped in luxury they had become spoilt bitches, black holes into which men had poured themselves, a malicious tribe of pinched faced princesses whose entire existence was devoted to the cult of themselves. And the more they were given the faster their descent into boredom. They lived in a world where nothing was ever good enough -- the car was too white, the spaghetti was too long, the time was too right. He wouldn't make the same mistake. Instead, every six months he would drip feed his harem with a canoe load of goodies bought in Manaus and ferried up river by Pacon. Nothing fancy; just pots and pans and the occasional roll of brightly coloured cloth. Oh how they would worship him. He would become a god, a magnet to every nubile female in the rainforest. And of course he would have to keep the men sweet. The last thing he wanted was a mutiny on his hands! A second canoe would have to be summoned, this one containing axe heads and chisels. Gradually, over time, he would introduce little luxuries such as whiskey for the men and chocolate for the women. Once they were hooked he would have total mastery over them. Soon other tribes would be amalgamated, enticed by stories of opulence and the promise of an easy life.

Slowly, deliciously, year on year, he would slide into the morass of sexual perversion, his despotic kingdom famed throughout the Amazon for its malformed offspring.

"Sir!!!"

An elbow dug into Nick's ribs. "Umm?" Pacon was staring at him.

"The chief wants to know if you are enjoying the food?"

"What?..........Oh it's marvellous! Really tasty, yes."

"You've hardly touched it! " said Daniel.

"I have! I'm just taking my time......Er, Pacon, please ask the chief if his tribe have come across any illegal logging recently."

Pacon consulted Trumac. There followed a brief discussion in *Arawak.*

'The chief says the loggers and getting closer to the village. He is very worried."

"Bloody criminals!"

Trumac clapped his hands. Six men wearing feathered headdresses entered the circle of light carrying various sized drums, the sides of which were studded with multi coloured beads. They sat down in an arc to the right of the fire and began to play. Slowly at first, the lone bass drum pounding out an incessant rhythm. The whole tribe fell silent, as if called to prayer. The drum beat echoed throughout the *Tabanau.* Its seismic effect was felt upon the ground, like the heartbeat of the earth. Soon the midrange drums joined in and the tempo increased. The tribe became agitated. They rose to their feet as one, shoulders and hips swaying. A third tier of drums redoubled the rhythm. Instantly the tribe responded. A chaotic fire dance broke out, a wild and crazy tableau of jerking, uncontrollable bodies. The men watched open mouthed. Daniel felt the visceral urge to stand up, to join in and abandon himself. But he stayed put, his English reserve pinning him to the ground. Ben's heart raced -- the forest of arms and legs fracturing the blazing firelight was like some ancient code pulsing through his brain, erasing Cheshire from his cerebral cortex and dragging him back to his roots. Giles sat transfixed -- dressed in a bear skin he was smashing a stone axe onto the head of a woolly mammoth. The beast reared up and let out a mighty roar, but Giles finished it off, jamming a sharpened stake into its eye. He looked at Nick and grinned manically. But Nick was too busy ogling his sixteen year old bride-to-be, her bronze body shimmering as she danced. Legs apart, hips vibrating, she was shaking her head wildly, lost in the hypnotic beat of the drums.

CHAPTER SEVEN

Daniel looked as though he was facing a firing squad. "You're not leaving us with this lot, surely?!"

"I have work to do in Manaus," said Pacon, pulling on his cowboy boots. "You'll be fine. See you in three weeks."

"Three weeks!"

Nick grabbed Daniel's arm. "What's the matter? Giles and I have travelled with them before."

He shook himself free. "No one told me!"

"*I* did! On the flight over to Rio! But you were too busy eyeing up that stewardess!"

"Liar!"

"You've never been interested in what goes on in the rainforest!"

"Well I am now!" Panic set in. "Anyway, we need Pacon to translate. We can't speak the language."

"We don't need to. The guides know the score."

"I am *not* spending three weeks in the jungle with those two savages!"

"What! You fucking ignoramus!"

"Daniel, it's fine," said Giles, trying to calm the situation. "They're nice people. Honestly!"

"Bollocks! Look at their teeth!"

Two of the tribe's finest herbalists -- Kinta and Mirim -- stood motionless next the smouldering embers of last night's fire. Both men were in their forties. Small and squat, they had painted faces and carried machetes. They listened to the angry voices with confused, nervous expressions.

"Look!" said Nick, lowering his voice, "You're freaking them out!"

"*I'M* freaking *THEM out!!!!*"

Nick lost his patience. "Go back to Manaus with Pacon then! Go on! Seeing as your frightened! Fly home back to Daddy! I knew this would happen! I knew it!"

Daniel was all set to do just that when he realised the consequences of returning home -- his father would know for certain he was a useless backslider and Sophie would think him a coward. He looked at Ben for support. Ben looked at the ground. He'd made a fool of himself. He picked up his rucksack, slinging it over his left shoulder. "Three *fucking* weeks!"

Before leaving, Pacon reassured Kinta and Mirim that all was well by making a crude joke in *Arawak* about two monkeys shitting on a snake. They bent double with laughter, repeating the punch line while glancing at Daniel. Pacon shook hands with everyone and left. Daniel felt a terrible sense of foreboding. He'd only ever been on one camping trip before -- to Lake Windermere when he was fourteen -- and that ended in disaster; he'd pitched his tent too close to the lake and got an early morning soaking from the bow wave of a passing speedboat.

The whole tribe gathered round to wish the party a safe and successful trip. Kinta and Mirim hugged their wives, stroking their hair and kissing their pretty faces. Nick was shocked at how young the women were -- barely fourteen. With Trumac leading the way they all filed out through the *Tabanau* and accompanied the men beyond the cultivated plots to the edge of the rainforest. Surrounding the encampment on all sides it was an awesome sight; a great green mass rising up into the sky A final benediction from the shaman and they were on their way. Once more they plunge into the canopy. Kinta and Mirim took the lead, slashing dense foliage with their razor sharp machetes. Nick was next in line, followed by Daniel, Ben and Giles.

They'd barely gone fifty metres before Daniel piped up, "How far is it?"

Ben almost burst out laughing. Nick prepared himself for Daniel's childish questions. He delivered a scholarly and deadpan, "We're heading to an area northeast of here. Recent field trips have discovered plants rich in beta-carbo........"

"How far is it?"

"Five days.....at least!"

"Five days!!"

Nick called a halt to the march. He spun round to face Daniel, chewing him out. "Right! Let's get one thing straight from the start shall we! We're in for a gruelling three weeks. So I don't want any whinging about how hot it is, how tired you are, how fucked off you're getting! Because you may as well go back right now. This trip's been planned for months, and I'm not having you spoiling it. Got it?"

Daniel had never been spoken to like that by a mere employee. It fazed him somewhat. "Blimey! That's told me."

Nick turned round, motioning to Kinta to proceed. They all walked on in silence. Daniel was so pissed off he took his place at the back of the line. To cheer himself up he thought about his father's death. He would be in charge of the company then. And what pleasure he'd have summoning Nick to his office and telling him his services were no longer required. Get the *fuck* out in other words! But all that depended on him inheriting the family business. Two major obstacles had to be surmounted before that joyous day. First, for the next three weeks he had to keep his head down, obeying Nick's orders and mucking in with the rest of them. Second, and more importantly, he had to win Sophie back; a difficult thing stuck in the middle of the rainforest. He took solace in the old adage 'absence makes the heart grow fonder.' Dear sweet Sophie. Was she thinking about him? He cast his mind back to all the times he'd taken her for granted -- romantic dinners where she'd gone out of her way to look lovely while he spent his time flirting with the waitresses; bars they'd visited where his wandering eye had infiltrated the cleavage of every passing female; a skiing holiday they once took in Kloisters where he'd shagged a trio of chalet maids. He had a lot to make up for. But he would try his damnedest. He vowed that if he won her back he'd never look at another woman again. Deep down he knew he was being unrealistic. But was he? Maybe he could change. Rod Stewart had. Trudging through the steaming tropical furnace he took out his mobile and stared at the screensaver. There was Sophie, smiling up at him, her darling green eyes sparkling with love. His inner core melted at the sight of her.

As the sun went down the decision was made to pitch camp in a clearing covered in leaf litter. A small stream babbled nearby. To Daniel -- decrepitly tired and rung with sweat -- it was Shangri-La. His knees buckled the moment Nick said, "Here'll do." He slumped down, his whole body aching, his shoulders stinging with Christ like lacerations from the straps of his rucksack. Hours ago he'd wanted to complain, but his love for Sophie had welded his mouth shut. Still, he was determined to get under Nick's skin for what he'd put him through. So he fell back onto the soft bed of waxy leaves and sighed. "I'm absolutely knackered!"

Ben followed suit. "Me too!"

So did Giles. "And me!"

They could have stopped an hour ago. But Nick wanted to make Daniel suffer. Suffer for the countless times he'd humiliated him; for the hundreds of beautiful women he'd slept with; for being born so amazingly rich and good looking no woman could resist. Now he had him exactly where he wanted. Three weeks -- he could have done with three years.

Daniel felt a shiver beneath his hips. There it was again. He put his hand under the leaves and felt something warm. A large snake suddenly shot out from under him. "Facking hell!!" He leapt to his feet as though electrocuted, watching horrified as it slithered under a bush. "Shit, man! It could have killed me!"

Nick was overjoyed. "Lesson one. When making camp, always clear the ground first."

The team went into action. While Kinta looked for firewood and Mirim went to collect water from the stream, Ben and Giles pushed away the leaves with their boots. Once the ground was clear Nick erected a quartet of igloo tents. Daniel stood there like a spare part. He felt Nick was ignoring him on purpose, just so he could tell his father what a lazy bastard he was. "Can I help?"

Nick seemed put out. "Er..... give Kinta a hand collecting wood if you like."

"Sure." Daniel joined Kinta at the edge of the clearing. During the search Kinta came across a small, nondescript plant that grew at the base of a tree. He lifted it from the soil carefully, snapped off the base, brushed clean the roots and began to chew them. Disgusting.

"What's for dinner?" shouted Daniel.

The reply came back. "Fillet steak and duaphinoise potatoes."

"Brilliant!"

"Just kidding," laughed Nick. "Rice and black beans."

By the time the fire was lit darkness was falling, the sky above their heads glowing like a furnace. As the colour drained away, one by one the stars came out until the whole sky glittered like mica. Daniel ate his meal in silence. While the rest of the men chatted amiably he stared at his watch. He pictured Sophie driving home from work in her little yellow *Clio.* The radio might be on and...........

"Didn't we, Daniel?"

"What?"

"Get pissed at last year's Christmas party?" asked Giles. "What was the name of that club we went to afterwards? You remember. You shagged one of the barmaids."

Collecting firewood was one thing, but he drew the line at cosy fireside chats, especially ones that reminded him of his playboy past. He got to his feet. "Don't remember. I'm off to bed. See you in the morning." He climbed into his tent and zipped up the flaps with two noisy jerks as if to say 'fuck'....'you!'

"Something I said," whispered Giles.

Nick's reaction was a disdainful shake of the head. In hushed tones he gestured to the men to lean in closer. "I know what this is about -- his ex, Sophie. Gotta be. Caught him staring at a picture of her today on his phone." He nodded, his eyes bulging with pleasure. In the flickering firelight his overzealous features looked monstrous, like a greedy giant in a child's picture book. "Devastated he is. Absolutely devastated."

"I'm not......"

"*Shush!!!*"

"Sorry!" whispered Ben........"I'm not surprised. She's an absolute babe."

All eyes slid towards the babe magnet, his tent glowing eerily from within like an alien pupa. They could see his hunched up shadow peering into the light of his iPhone.

"Look!" said Nick. "He's at it again."

Giles shook his head. "Poor sod."

"Poor sod my arse. He's had it coming."

* * *

Day followed day. The same monotonous routine -- up at dawn, breakfast, break camp, trudge mile after mile through the sweltering heat, stop for lunch, drink water and chew on strips of dried meat and even drier biscuits, carry on trudging until the sun slipped below the canopy, find a suitable place to camp, make a fire, eat, go to bed -- the entire backbreaking regime under Nick's austere, dictatorial gaze. Daniel was sick to the back teeth of giant spiders, leaf cutter ants, exotic birds and howler monkeys. The arduous terrain really took it out of him. He'd lost half a stone and his legs and arms were covered in insect bites. His only respite at the end of a gruelling day was to retire to his tent and stare at Sophie's photo. Now he knew what the Tommies in the trenches had gone through. But he had to limit this indulgence to a mere two minutes; the last thing he wanted was for the battery to run out.

On the evening of day six, when it seemed the death march would last forever, Nick poked the fire with a long branch and informed everyone, "We should get to the research area tomorrow."

"Thank fuck for that!" exclaimed Daniel

Nick ignored him. "We'll set up permanent camp and spend the week collecting specimens. I've got high hopes for this particular area. It lies in valley not far from here. I recently read an article in Science and Nature that said............"

Daniel zoned out. All he could thing about was Sophie. Two more weeks in this hell hole and he'd be on his way home!

They broke camp at dawn and headed due east. Over the past few days the group had formed itself into three loose cliques -- Nick and Mirim strolling along in front, followed by Ben and Giles, with Daniel and Kinta loitering at the rear. Despite the herbalists complete lack of English, Nick and Daniel used them to unburden themselves.

Midway through the morning Nick and Mirim stopped for a water break. Nick sat down on a fallen log, wiped his brow, sighed and looked about him. "You're so lucky living here."

Here we go again! thought Mirim. Even though he didn't understand a word of what Nick was saying, he could tell by his hangdog expression and the drone of his voice that he was in for another dollop of self pity.

"So, so lucky. All those women back at your village. I bet *they're* not complicated are they? I bet *they* don't walk round thinking their God's gift. Not like the women in England......Bloody mercenaries they are. I tell you, Mirim, a good heart gets you nowhere with those bitches. All they're interested is what they can get out of you. Money money money.........I'd swap places with you any day. I mean, that wife of yours....how old is she, fourteen? Oh my God! I can only imagine what *that* must be like!"

Daniel too was off on one. He was standing behind a huge moss covered boulder showing Kinta the photo of Sophie for the umpteenth time.

"I mean *look* at her......Don't you think she's lovely?.........I miss her so much......Fucked up big time I did......Thing is, it wasn't actually *my* fault. The bitch giving me the blow *knew* I was engaged. I'd just announced it for God's sake!........I'm determined to win her back.......Life's hell without her."

By now Nick was approaching his nadir. "I'm so lonely. You've no idea.....The nights are the worst. Cry myself to sleep sometimes........I mean, why can't I meet someone? Is it too much to ask?.......I've thought about suicide you know. Oh yes!......Anyway, come on. We've got work to do."

Daniel shook his head. "Women! They chew you up and spit you out. We're better off without them."

Suddenly Nick's voice rang out up ahead. "OH MY GOD!!!! QUICK! EVERYONE! OVER HERE! OH DEAR GOD IN HEAVEN!!!!"

"What does that prick want now!?" Daniel and Kinta sprinted off down a narrow pathway. They bumped into Ben and Giles. "What's going on?"

"Dunno," said Giles.

All four scrambled through dense foliage towards the panic stricken voice. They broke cover and saw Nick standing at the edge of a plateau. Shoulders slumped, he was staring dejectedly into the valley below.

"What's going on?" shouted Daniel. "You're frightening the wildlife!"

"There's no wildlife to frighten."

"What are you talking about?"

Nick pointed dead ahead. Daniel, Giles and Ben approached the edge of the precipice. They gazed down into the valley. As far as the eye could see, from horizon to horizon, the forest had been uprooted, slashed and burnt. All that remained was a parched landscape of charred tree stumps churned up by caterpillar tracks. In the far distance, beneath a pall of smoke, men the size of ants were loading massive logs onto a line of flatbed trucks.

It had arrived. The moment Daniel had been waiting for. After days of being ordered around -- fetch this, carry that -- he was now presented with the perfect opportunity for revenge. Not just for the past week, either. For years this bald nonentity had made his life a misery; droning on and on at endless meetings. Then hearing his father laud him to the rooftops, saying he was the 'finest research chemist in Britain.' He wasn't *that* good. He couldn't even get a girlfriend! All Daniel's nihilism -- stored up from the day his mother walked out and fuelled by a spineless father who had given him everything -- poured forth in one tiny word. He walked over to where Nick was slumped, looked again at the scarred and smouldering valley, and said, flippantly........"So?"

Behind the prison bars of his hands the word slammed bullet like into Nick's brain. He lifted his head slowly. The greedy giant had morphed into a terrifying ogre -- all snarling eyes and grimacing teeth. "*So?.....SO!!!* An area the size of London's been wiped out and all you can say is 'So'!........You don't understand, do you? This is our *research* area! And it's all been destroyed!"

"Well you'll just have to find another one then, won't you!"

"There *isn't* another one! This is it; the end of the expedition!"

"Bollocks! Ask the Indians! They must know plenty of places!"

"I have! This is the only area that contains the trees and shrubs we're looking for!"

"D'you mean to say I've spent a week of my life trudging through this shit hole for nothing?"

"Shit hole! *Shit hole!* This beautiful wilderness containing every remedy known to man?"

"That's bollocks and you know it! Most of the drugs are synthesised in the lab these days!"

"Most of the *known* drugs are! What about the unknown ones? Whose going to discover them when the rainforest has gone?"

The rainforest again! He was sick of hearing about it. A smirk was called for. "I'll be long dead by then."

Nick was staggered. "You spoilt bastard!"

Daniel winced. Only his father dared call him that. A line had been crossed. Their relationship had gone beyond mere sarcasm. It was war. He steamed in, grabbing Nick's collar. "Listen, you bald cretin. I couldn't give a shit if they bulldozed the whole lot and turned it into a car park!"

Nick smashed his forehead into Daniel's nose. He staggered back, clasping his hands to his face. Blood poured through his fingers. "You broke my nose you *bastard!!"*

"Good! Wait till your father hears about this!"

He lunged at Nick. Fists, punches and kicks flew. Giles grabbed Daniel round the shoulders, pulling him away.

"Get off me! I'll kill the fucker!!"

Giles hung on. "For God's sake, Daniel! Calm down! Things are bad enough as it is!"

Standing a few meters away Kinta and Mirim ignored the squabbling white men.

Instead, with great sadness they stared out across the raped and pillaged valley.

Later that night Daniel was exiled in his tent while the rest of the men gathered round the campfire. He could hear the crackle of logs and the murmur of conversation. Using the back of a metal plate as a mirror he examined his swollen face in its dull, pitted surface, angling it left and right. Then he heard something that made his blood run cold.

"Are you *really* going to resign when you get back?" asked Ben, in an upbeat tone that betrayed his desire to climb the company ladder (for weeks his girlfriend had been going on about this handsome hunk who worked in her office. Rich he was. Stinking. And he was always chatting her up). Ben was desperate to keep her. A fabulous weekend for two in Paris to celebrate his stellar promotion would do it, crowned by a casual slip of the tongue over dinner revealing his massive salary increase.

Nick's voice rang loud and clear. "Too right! He's not getting away with this!"

Daniel's sphincter puckered. He pictured the scene in his father's office. "He's resigned! The finest research chemist in the country! What the *hell* were you playing at!"

"But Dad! Look what he did to my face!"

"Your *face* is persona non grata as far as I'm concerned! Now get out of my office! You're no longer my son!"

Another nail thudded into the coffin. He heard Nick announce, chillingly, "I could walk into any pharmaceutical company tomorrow....unlike someone I could mention."

Oh shit! thought Daniel. Who's gonna employ me?

The trek back to the Atori village was a fractious affair. Daniel and Nick could barely look at one another, so Nick spent the day up front with Mirim. His vicious head butt had given him a hero's euphoria. He, spindly Nick, had dared to stand up to that rugby paying thug. Not only that, he'd broken his nose! Mirim was quick to notice a change in his behaviour. Now and then Nick tapped him on the shoulder, asked for the machete and took over the hacking duties. Even the tone of his voice had altered from downbeat to up.

Daniel skulked at rear with Kinta. When Mirim's slashing blade ceased to slash and everyone stopped for a break, Daniel hung back, keeping Kinta with him. It was on day nine, two days after the brawl, that Daniel's curiosity was finally aroused. They'd stopped near a picturesque waterfall when, as usual, Kinta uprooted the same nondescript plant he'd been chewing on since the start of the expedition.

Daniel sat down on a rock and beckoned him over. He pointed at the plant, shrugging his shoulders to suggest confusion. "What's......*that*?"

It took a few seconds for Kinta to understand. Then it dawned on him; his two year old son did the same thing when confronted with a strange object for the first time. He lifted up the plant and smiled. "Chamcha."

"Cham what?"

"Cham-cha."

"Chamcha......Oh, right." He pointed at the roots. Using his miming skills he pretended to snap a piece off and eat it. Then he shrugged his shoulders again and asked, "Why.....you.....*eat!*.....Chamcha?"

Kinta was quick to catch on. "Wo-ma."

Daniel frowned. "Wo-ma? Fuck are you talking about, 'Wo-ma'?"

Kinta picked up a stick, smoothed the ground with the sole of his foot and began to draw the outline of stick woman with large breasts.

"Woman!.....You mean *woman*!"

Kinta nodded back, delighted. "*Si!.....Si!......*Woman!"

Daniel pointed at the plant. "But what's *that.........*got to do with," he then pointed at the stick woman..."*that?*"

Kinta drew three triangles, each with a door. "Kinta home."

"Home?..........You mean your village? Vill-age?"

"*Si.* Vill-age." He pointed again at the stick woman. "Wo-man in vill-age."

Daniel nodded. "Woman in village. Right."

Kinta pointed at himself. "Kinta no vill-age."

"I see. Woman in village, you not in village. Go on."

"No....." Kinta pointed at the plant..... "chamcha. Kinta......." He then drew a stick man with a huge erect phallus.

A laddish grin spread across Daniel's his face. "You randy sod! So whenever you're away from your village." He pointed at the plant......"chamcha stops you thinking about......" He pointed at the erect phallus......."sex?"

Kinta nodded. "*Sex. Si!*"

"Really!?"

Kinta then drew a crude heart and brain on the stick man. He crossed out the phallus. "No." Crossed out the heart. "No." Crossed out the brain. "No."

The enormity of what Kinta was suggesting suddenly dawned on him. "*NO!*"

"*Si,* chamcha!"

Daniel picked up the plant nervously. He could hardly believe what he was about to say. "So......so this plant not only stops you thinking about sex.......it stops you thinking about women full stop?"

Kinta sensed Daniel's excitement. He grinned, nodding his head. "Chamcha!"

Daniel jumped to his feet and started pacing up and down. "Fucking hell! Fucking hell! I need to try this." He popped one of the roots in his mouth, chewing hard and swallowing it down. It had a pleasant aftertaste of liquorice. He took out his mobile and was about to switch it on.

"No!" exclaimed Kinta, gesturing for him to wait.

Famed for his impatience, it was the longest wait of Daniel's life. After ten minutes Kinta motioned to him that it was OK. Trembling, he powered up his phone. Up popped the photo of Sophie, smiling serenely. He stared at her angelic face. Expecting the same gut wrenching sense of loss and worthlessness, instead a strange and wonderful calm descended. He closed his eyes for a few seconds, then opened them again.........Nothing. He may as well have been looking at a photo of a goat. "Oh my God!.........*Oh my GOD!!!!!!*"

He screamed so loud a flock of parakeets exploded out of the tress and set off squawking. Up ahead, Nick heard the commotion and doubled back. He met up with Giles and Ben. "Was that Daniel? What's he done now!" They set off down the track. "Daniel! Daniel!"

Daniel heard them approach. Desperate to keep the discovery to himself he pleaded with Kinta, "Kinta, friend!" He pointed at the plant and shook his head. "No Chamcha!"

Kinta understood. He put his finger to his lips. "*Si,* no chamcha."

"Cheers, I owe you one."

Nick, Giles and Ben came running towards them. "What's happened?" asked Nick.

Daniel remained ice cool. "Nothing......I er...... I stood on a thorn, that's all."

* * *

Three days later they arrived back at the Atori village. Immediately Trumac sent word upriver that the *gringos* had returned earlier than expected. The next morning Pacon appeared with a fresh bruise on his face. "So, not a successful trip then?"

"No!" said Nick sharply. "A complete shambles!"

Speak for yourself, thought Daniel. During the past few days his mind had been fixated by one thing and one thing only -- his amazing discovery. A complete change had come over him. Instead of skulking about not speaking, he couldn't have been more amiable, cracking jokes with Ben and helping with the camp chores. At certain moments of the day he would burst out laughing for no reason. But it was at night that the biggest change took place. Ensconced in his tent peering into his iPhone, he giggled like a madman. Nick put it down to jungle fever, a mythical condition known to affect white men new to the tropics. But Daniel's mind couldn't have been clearer, his thoughts more precise. If chamcha could be synthesised into tablet form then the possibilities were limitless. Finally Man could free himself from female dependency. And what a wonderful world it would be! First though, he would have to test it out. And there was no place on earth better suited to such an exhaustive test than the sexual hotbed that was Rio de Janeiro. If it worked there, it would work anywhere!

"We're leaving in half an hour," said Nick. "Get your stuff together."

Daniel had some last minute stocking up to do. He took Kinta part way into the forest, took off his *Breitling* and gave it to him. "This is for you. Take it." He pointed to the myriad plants growing on the forest floor. "Need more chamcha."

Kinta was dumbstruck by the watch. "*Si!* Chamcha!"

They wandered round, scanning the undergrowth. Daniel thought he recognised the plant, but every time he went to pick it Kinta shook his head. "No chamcha!" Kinta then astounded him by picking an almost identical plant nearby, exclaiming, "Chamcha!"

"Bloody hell! They all look the same to me."

He just couldn't get the hang of it. Finally, when his rucksack was full, he heard Nick's voice shouting inside the *Tabanau.* "Daniel! Where are you? We're ready to leave!"

Daniel was about to set off when a frightening thought came to him. He grabbed Kinta's arm. "Kinta! Kinta! ....Chamcha? Good for wo-man?"

Kinta grinned, shaking his head. "Chamcha no good. Make wo-man sick."

"Bonus!"

"Where the *hell* is he!" said Nick. "Typical! Fucking typical!"

"Here he is," said Giles.

It got on Nick's nerves they way Daniel strolled towards them with a stupid smirk on his face. He acted like he didn't have a care in the world!

Daniel puffed out both cheeks and winked at Ben. "That was one hell of a shit."

"You'll be in the shit when we get back," said Nick.

"You don't frighten me, you little prick. Resign or not, makes no difference now."

They said their goodbyes to the tribe. Paddling upriver in the six man canoe Pacon explained that, instead of spending the night at his shack, he would drive them straight back to Manaus. It was far better all round, he said. Comfortable beds awaited them at their hotel near the airport. And besides, gentlemen such as themselves shouldn't have to sleep in fly blown shacks. What he didn't say was, the mouse had threatened to pound his head with the skillet if he even *thought* about bringing them back. And just in case he didn't believe her -- *Cloink!* -- there was one to be going one with.

Daniel was sitting directly behind Nick. As the canoe floated upstream amidst the magnificent jungle scenery, he leaned forward and whispered in his ear, "You were right about one thing, Slater. Cure for everything in the rainforest."

CHAPTER EIGHT

Daniel stared through the oval plexiglass, its tipping perspective. A sequence of curved beaches -- Botafogo, Flamengo, Copacabana, Ipanema -- scrolled into view. Down there, on those blinding white sands, beautiful women lay toasting in the sun. He hadn't taken chamcha for over 24 hours, purposely withholding it from his system, and already he could feel the first twinges in his groin. Mother Nature was sharpening her claws. He sat back in his seat, ruminating. How come everything wants to fuck everything else? Over and over again it was going on. Right this second, in every city, forest and ocean around the globe, something was seeking something else out to fuck. A millisecond's orgasm and the endless pantomime would begin again. And for what? Daniel couldn't figure it out. He rested his foot on the comforting bulk of his rucksack. God willing, the treasure wrenched from her diabolical laboratory would negate that ravenous appetite. Thoughts of Sophie seeped into his brain. Feelings flooded back. Powerful things, feelings. They make you do stupid things, like work all the hours God sends so you can spend your life with someone who ends up hating your guts. Spunking your money away just to be humiliated. Because anything is better than living alone........That was it! He'd finally worked it out! A feeling of intense joy swept over him. He felt ecstatic, liberated. Stupid, spoilt Daniel, the man whose father called him a useless waste of space, had uncovered a truth that had perplexed philosophers for centuries. Socrates, Plato, Aristotle......none of them had a clue. Only he, Daniel, had found the one true answer, the universal panacea. And it was right there in his rucksack.

The taxi ride to the Othon Palace was excruciating. He had to watch as one captivating women after another strolled along the tessellated sidewalks, their hips shimmering beneath their sarongs. He would have gladly spent the rest of his life with every single one of them. Driving along the *Avenida Atlantica,* Copacabana beach to his left, he worked himself up into such a state that he bent down and began to tear open the straps of his rucksack. But then the taxi pulled up in front of the hotel. Without saying a word he flung open the door and rushed into the foyer.

"Oh, right" said Nick. "It's like that is it."

Daniel burst into his room, nerves shredded. He could hear voices coming from the balcony next door. Americans by the sound of it. A man and a woman. "Hey, babe!" the man shouted. "Check out the view!" Typical. One more shmuck on Nature's merry-go-round. He imagined him wining and dining Babe a few weeks back, pulling out the brochure and showing her where they were staying. She, cooing, "Oh Matt, it must have cost a fortune!" He, puffed up with macho pride, "You're so worth it, babe."

Daniel threw his rucksack onto the bed. He caught sight of the telephone on a side table. Why not pick it up and speak to Sophie? *Go on, she's waiting for you.* His heart was racing. His hands shook. He pulled open the rucksack, removed one of the miracle plants and hurried into the bathroom, turning on the tap. He gave the roots a good rinse before cramming them into his mouth. He crunched down hard, chewing them over and over before swallowing them in one gulp. He rushed back into the room and sat on the bed, waiting. He closed his eyes." Please may this work, God. Please!"

One by one the puppet strings dissolved. His breathlessness subsided, his heartbeat decreased, his agitated thoughts dwindled to a balanced and peaceful rationale. All that frustration, all that longing had vanished. He opened his eyes. Nature no longer had her claws in him. Free from the insatiable urge to procreate, he felt a deep sense of calm. He stared at Sophie's photo.

Nothing. But the ultimate test lay ahead -- Copacabana Beach. He got up off the bed and walked out onto the balcony. There it was, stretched out before him, dazzling in the sun. If he could resist its sensual treasures then surely anything was possible. The American woman from next door suddenly appeared on the balcony. She was a ravishing brunet in her mid twenties wearing a lime green bikini that accentuated her luscious curves.

"Oh! Hi!" she said, staring into his eyes, anticipating them devouring her body.

He barely gave her a second look, walking back indoors.

"Fag," she said, under her breath.

He realised that Nature wouldn't give up without a fight. She would exploit his weaknesses, titillate his fancy, utilise every weapon in her vast armoury. So he grabbed another root, stuffed it into his pocket just in case and took the lift down to foyer. He strolled across the marble floor, readying himself for the coming battle. Slipping on his designer sunglasses he took a deep breath, walked outside and crossed the *Avenida.* It wasn't long before the first salvo was deployed. Standing at a beachside bar a cute sixteen year old was sipping coconut milk through a straw, puckering her lips as she did so, tipping her head foreword and gazing at him with sweet beguiling eyes. Slowly her greedy mouth released the straw. A trickle of milk dribbled down her chin. 'Oops!' her eyes said, as she flicked out her tongue to lap it up. Nothing. When he set foot on the sand he found a cluster of landmines strewn in his path -- a group of topless twenty somethings gathered to celebrate a friend's birthday. As he past, one of them squirted suntan oil over her naked breasts. She put the bottle down and with both hands began slip slopping the glistening liquid. Nothing. In no-man's-land he encountered eight bikini-clad missiles playing beach volleyball. Tall and athletic, three were blonde while the other five had inky black warheads. At the start of each point they all crouched down, pushing out their sumptuous payloads, waiting for the server to launch the ball across the net. The server, teeing up the ball in her left hand, shook the sweat from her tousled hair, squinted into the sun, arched her back serenely and scolded the ball with a satisfying thwack. Nothing. Finally he was in the thick of it. Regiments of beautiful women lay prostrate on the sand, each with their own state-of-the-art weaponry. Some were languid, with delicately carved features and mournful expressions; others had full blown pneumatic lips and breasts, replete in silicon splendour. Strolling along the shoreline still more lay in wait -- tigerish, calculating sluts with salacious eyes; shy, butter-wouldn't-melt maidens sexy in their doleful innocence -- a captivating potpourri guaranteed to frazzle the brain and swell the glands. And scattered amongst all this live ammunition were the spent cartridges of yesteryear; old women with sagging breasts and thighs, war horses from previous campaigns whose conquests had long since been shipped off to the cemetery. Mother Nature, up to date with the latest internet perversions, had brought these battle axes out of retirement to fulfil the fantasies of her ever growing band of granny shaggers. In fact there were no depths she wouldn't plumb in her frantic effort to procreate. And if a few freaks were born along the way, so be it! It was all part of life's rich tapestry. None of them would go to waste, the Dark Web would see to that.

She threw everything at him along that beach, her last throw of the dice two stunning lesbians French kissing in the surf..........Nothing. It was as if he was walking down the aisle of a supermarket, its produce barely registering. His was total victory.

For aeons she had waged all out war on the male sex, tempting them, frustrating them. Now, finally, he had found a way to strike back. He had discovered her Achilles heel deep within the rainforest. Such was her female arrogance she had grown this plant out of sheer bravado, right under the noses of men, laughing at their follies, and like some monstrous Miss Havirsham she had gloried in their downfall. But now her secret was out, and Daniel was determined to use it against her. And just in time by the look of it! Walking back towards the *Avenida* he witnessed the most terrifying sight of all -- hoards of mini minxes playing in the sand. The equipment had yet to arrive, the reactor not yet switched on, but there they were, these prepubescent putti, lying in wait for the next generation, each darling cherub tailor made to lead a man to destruction. He surveyed the conquered beach with a haughty smile. This miracle plant would liberate men from the shackles of sexual dependency, where too much was never enough and where never enough prompted thoughts of suicide. It would earn him billions. Trillions! And in the process the Nobel Prize for chemistry.

"Champagne. Cristal." Back at the hotel Daniel eased himself onto a barstool.

The barman nodded, dipping below the curved marble topped bar. Four seats along the American couple were enjoying a late afternoon cocktail. He was all over her, a blanket of smarm. Producing a small leather box from his jacket pocket he said, "Got you this, babe. I know how much you like rubies."

Babe preened, prising open the lid. Two heart shaped earrings dazzled. "Oh, Matt! They're.....they're.........!" She threw her arms around him. "I love you so much!"

The barman placed the ice bucket on the bar and grinned. Lucky guy. She was a real beauty. He carried on grinning as he undid the gold foil, popped the cork and poured out the drink.

The sound prompted Matt to say, "Hey, barman! We'll have one of those!"

Babe squeezed his arm. "Let's not drink too much, honey. We've had four cocktails already."

"You're right.......Barman. Cancel that."

Daniel sipped his champagne serenely, watching as the two lovebirds left the bar arm in arm. And neither did his pulse race when a high class hooker slipped her sumptuous bottom onto the stool next to him. She wore the tiniest of miniskirts that rode up as she crossed her long tanned legs. She leaned forward, exposing her cleavage. Daniel studied her with the cold eye of a scientist. Framed by a curtain of strawberry blonde hair her angelic, wilful face was orchestrated by a sensual mouth that glistened as she spoke. "Hi." Her voice had a dusky timbre, her cobalt blue eyes rich and penetrating. He was about to get up and walk out when an idea came to him. He called the barman over. "Get me another glass will you." Once again the barman grinned.

As the champagne was being poured Daniel turned to the hooker. "How much?"

"Five hundred US dollars."

Wow! She must be good. "You're hired. Meet me here at seven forty five."

Daniel went back to his room and picked up the phone. "Put me through to room 306..........Hi, Nick. It's Daniel.......Nothing's the matter....... Look, I know this trip's been a disaster, but we might as well end it on a civilised note. Join me for dinner. My shout..........OK, great. Let's meet in the restaurant at eight."

Nick chuckled as he replaced the receiver. So, the spoilt bastard wanted a truce, did he? It was obvious why. He was scared stiff of what his father would do when he got back. Nick had waited a long time for this moment. Perhaps he should go round head butting more people. One thing was for sure, the moment big mouth Giles told everyone at work about his tremendous assault on the boss's son his sexual stock would rise. Violence in the jungle! What a turn on! He'd no longer be thought of as a wimp. Now every woman at Page Pharmaceuticals would want to sleep with him. Who knows, maybe his luck was about to change!

7.30 found Daniel in the bathroom chopping up a freshly washed root of chamcha. He tipped the broken pieces into a small plastic bag, slipping it into his jacket pocket.

Strolling into the bar he saw the high class hooker waiting for him. She wore a tight purple dress, her blonde hair gathered up in loose ringlets. She was a real beauty this one. No doubt about it. Her presence sent a thrill of expectation through the dozen or so men sitting in the bar with their wives and girlfriends. The women on the other hand flashed jealous stares in her direction -- What a tart! What a whore! -- every single one of them envious of her God given loveliness.

Daniel bought her a cocktail and revealed his plan. "He's not the best looking guy on the planet, so you're really going to earn your money." Close up he could smell her perfume, a bewitching fragrance combining subtle notes of jasmine and rose. Thank God he'd taken chamcha.

She fixed him with the determined stare of a gold digger about to wed a billionaire forty years her senior. "So long as I get my money I don't give a shit."

"Good. He might be a bit reluctant, so give it your best shot."

The insult stung her feminine pride. "Reluctant!" Her eyes flashed around the contours of her body. "*Senhor!* No man alive can resist *this!* Believe me, I know!"

Daniel smirked. "We'll see. Anyway, he's in room 306. I'm in 502. Come and see me when you've finished. I want to hear every last detail." He counted out $250 in crisp fifties. "Half now, half later." Placing the notes in her hand he noticed her expression; it was one of complete rapture. She was staring at the money with all the devotion of a Renaissance Madonna gazing at the infant Christ. He glanced to his left and saw Nick emerge from the lift and walk across the foyer towards the restaurant; his tense, agitated gait testament to years of sexual frustration. "That's him there!"

"Ughhh!"

"Told you. And remember, I want you to try."

"Try!"

Nick was led to a table for two by a petite waitress in her late thirties with short dark hair and a friendly smile. "Can I get you a drink, sir?" He particularly liked the way she lowered her eyes when she spoke. The fact he'd been invited out by a subservient Daniel instilled in him a Bond like confidence, his incredible head butt fuelling his self esteem. He picked up the napkin and threw it casually across his lap. "Scotch. No ice." He was about to ask her what she was doing later but aborted at the last second.

Si, Senhor. Any particular brand?"

This threw him. He didn't drink Scotch. "Er.....Teachers."

No! He didn't imagine it! As she turned away just then she held his gaze for a split second, the cutest of grins lighting up her oval face. Yes!!!! Oh shit. Here comes Daniel. The waitress was bound to fancy him. Maybe not. Perhaps she wasn't the shallow type. Perhaps she could see past his good looks. Daniel pulled up a chair and sat down. "Evening."

The petite waitress reappeared, addressing Daniel. "Can I get you a drink, sir?"

"Rum and coke."

"*Si.*"

Amazing! She didn't even give him a second look!

"Where are Ben and Giles tonight?" asked Daniel.

"They've gone to the Maracana. Local derby evidently........Mindless rubbish."

Daniel picked up the menu and gave a philosophical shrug. "We're going home tomorrow. Any plans?"

Nick was wary of his opening gambit. "What do you mean?"

"We didn't find what we were looking for, so.........."

"We'll just have to come back next year."

For his plan to succeed he had to put Nick at his ease. "Not me. I'll leave it to the experts. One thing this trip has taught me, I'm no lover of the great outdoors. Yep, think I'll stick to the office in future."

Self deprecation! Blimey! This was new. And also, *ALSO!* that cute waitress was staring over. "Each to his own."

Brilliant! The mug was taking it up the arse. He noticed during the soft soaping that Nick kept glancing at the waitress. "You're in there."

"Do you think so?"

"Definitely."

Flushed crimson Nick grabbed the menu, his eyes flitting from starters to waitress.

"Order what you want, mate. On me."

'Mate'! He must really be shitting himself! "Cheers, Daniel. I'll have the steak."

Boring bastard. "Good choice......Yep, I reckon that waitress fancies you. Not bad is she?" He summoned her over and ordered the food. "And bring us a bowl of salad as well would you."

And with all the subtlety of an expert lover Daniel plied Nick with the most expensive wines. The more he drank the more he relaxed and flirted with the waitress. The little dwarf was a mere aperitif to the gargantuan feast that awaited upstairs.

"Try the salad, Nick. It's delicious." He watched him take the bait and dig his fork into the bowl of greenery. "Hang on! Isn't that Lewis Hamilton over there?"

"Where?"

"There. Checking in at reception. Looks like him."

As Nick turned and squinted into the foyer, Daniel whipped out the plastic bag and emptied the chamcha into the salad, mixing it in rapidly. "Oh no. My mistake. Thought for a minute it was."

Nick turned back to the table and began to consume the salad. "Umm. See what you mean, Daniel. It's got a nice liquorice taste to it. Unusual. Thanks for recommending it."

"My pleasure." An uneasy fear suddenly gripped him. Nick hadn't had a girlfriend for years. Say the drug had no effect on his raging libido? What then? He'd be finished. No, the drug *would* work. His stroll along Copacabana beach proved it. And look, already he was taking no notice of the waitress, despite her constant glances. "Hey, Nick. That waitress can't take her eyes off you."

Nick gave her a cursory look. He carried on munching, his thoughts elsewhere.

It's working! Wait, wait; the dwarf was one thing, the high class hooker something else.

Nick finished off the salad and emptied his glass of wine.

"Pudding?" asked Daniel.

"No, thanks. Think I'll have an early night."

"Nothing wrong is there?"

"No, no. I feel great. Very er......." Nick got to his feet. "Thanks for the meal."

Daniel watched him stroll out of the restaurant, a man at peace with himself, completely ignoring the flirting waitress. How ironic, thought Daniel -- the first time in years a woman had come on to him and his system was full of chamcha.

Nick pushed open the door to his room. He felt a strange sense of calm. Perhaps it was the wine. He walked out onto the balcony and looked down at the swimming pool three storeys below. A busty red head he'd spied earlier was emerging from the water after a long swim. She grabbed the handrail and climbed out. Scooping back her hair she sauntered to her sun lounger, lay down and began smothering her body in tanning oil. Nick's attention was diverted to a flock of sparrows pecking poolside crumbs. It amused him the way they fluttered about in a sort of chaotic dance. They had slightly different markings to the ones in Britain. And one was slightly bigger. Oh yes, it was some sort of finch. He walked back inside and switched on the TV. One of those *novellas* came on where a scantily clad secretary was finally giving herself to her boss. Smiling, she popped the buttons of his shirt one by one. He switched over to a documentary about Brazil's largest sugarcane refinery. He lay down on the bed, propping himself up on a pillow, marvelling at the sheer scale of the operation; the gleaming stainless steel vats and endless network of piping. When it finished he switched channels to a football match screened live from the Maracana. Giles and Ben are there tonight, thought Nick. What *do* they see in it? Football was a stupid game played and watched by idiots. But that was a clever bit of skill just then, the way that black player lifted the ball over his opponents head. The crowd agreed, with a roar. He found himself leaning over and removing a beer from the mini bar, not taking his eyes off the screen. A knock came at the door. He padded across the parquet floor and opened it.

The high class hooker smouldered in the doorway. "Hi, I'm staying across the hall. I've lost my room key. Is it possible I could use your bathroom?"

"Of course. Come in."

She entered, brushing his arm lightly with tips of her manicured fingers. "Really kind of you. Are you in Rio on business?"

"Sort of. I'm a research chemist, not that you're interested."

"No! No! I am! Tell me more!" Her seductive blue eyes stared at him in limpid fascination.

"Well, I er........"

She squeezed his wrist. "Pour us both a drink while I use the bathroom. Then you can tell me all about it."

"If you want."

She glanced at the bed. "Go on, relax. I won't be long."

He watched her vanish into the bathroom, closing the door with a mischievous grin. Nick did as he was told. He sat on the bed and opened the mini bar. But instead of choosing the bottle of champagne he pulled out another beer. A roar from the TV told him a goal had been scored. He watched the replay -- that skilful black player again, he'd dribbled past three defenders and chipped the ball over the goalkeeper. Now it was one all with only fifteen minutes to go! Bloody hell! Giles and Ben were certainly getting their money's worth!

The bathroom door creaked open. Slowly, seductively, the high class hooker walked towards the bed, the air crackling with static generated by the sexy swish of her nylons. She stood in front of the TV, and with a dreamy fluidity eased down the straps of her dress, letting it fall to the floor. Caressed in a lacy black bra, stockings and suspenders, her voluptuous body was breathtaking. Flesh and bone had never been carved with such dazzling virtuosity -- a heavenly hourglass sculpted from the finest honey coloured flesh. She undid the fastenings to her hair, loosening a cascade of ringlets. And with her tiny hands she enveloped both breasts, pushing them together and pouting, "Fuck me."

* * *

Daniel lay on the bed thrumming the duvet with his fingers. He'd watched her go up in the lift ten minutes ago and wondered what was going on in room 306. All sorts of scenarios flashed through his mind -- Nick feasting on her body, sucking the life out of it; soaping her breasts in the shower, tonguing her nipples, demanding all sorts of blow jobs. Then a truly horrific scene -- denied sex for so long he was strangling her with her stockings, straining with all his might, his intense bloodshot face inches from hers. And then, certain that life was extinguished, masturbating over her stunning corpse.

Two brisk taps at the door. Room service! To calm his nerves Daniel had phoned down and ordered a bottle of scotch. It was going to be a long night. "Come in!"

Instead of a bottle wielding waiter the high class hooker walked in. She was distraught. "I've never been so *insulted* in my life!"

"Oh God, he didn't attack you did he? I was going to warn you about that."

She slipped off her dress, revealing her perfect body that since the age of fourteen had so hypnotised the male sex. "I offered him this! *THIS!!!!* And do you know what he did?.........He didn't even *look* at me! He just sat there watching TV!"

"Really!?"

"Then he started laughing, closed his eyes and said 'freedom'."

"'Freedom'! It gets better and better!" Daniel was ecstatic. He took out three hundred dollars from his wallet and gave them to her. "Here's the balance, plus a fifty dollar tip. You don't know how happy you've made me."

Once she'd counted the money the hooker calmed down. She quite fancied Daniel, and had an hour to kill before her next client. She coiled her arms around his waist. "How about it? You *have* paid!"

"No thanks. Need an early night."

Raging, she snatched her dress off the floor and put it on. "It's true what they say about the English! You're all gay!" She hurried out and slammed the door.

Daniel did a little jig, punching the air. Then he stopped. "'Gay?' Oh shit! It doesn't make you gay does it?"

He heard the American guy on the balcony. "Just popping the towel out to dry, babe."

Daniel steeled himself and walked outside. "Evening."

Matt was wearing boxer shorts and drooping a large white towel over the balcony rail. "Oh, hi."

Daniel stared at his muscular body, his eyes wandering over mountainous abs and pecs. Matt scowled and walked straight back inside. "You're right about that English guy, babe! Solid gold faggot!"

Daniel looked up at the stars. "Not a twitch! Thank you God!"

* * *

Rio International Airport was strangely quiet. It seemed to match Nick's mood. While Ben was sitting in the departure lounge texting his girlfriend, he and Giles were scanning a row of magazines. Nick cringed as came across the latest copy of *Esquire.* Kelly Brook, wearing lacy black lingerie, was staring at him with her captivating come-to-bed eyes. He reached out and touched the glossy cover. A body equal to this if not better was on a plate for him last night, yet he'd refused. Laughed even! A once-in-a-lifetime women like that! He would never, ever forgive himself.

"Fancy Daniel getting a limo to the airport," said Giles. "You'd think he'd have given us a lift! I don't know what's wrong him. He was as happy as Larry over breakfast. I wouldn't like to be in his shoes when he gets back! Probably thought fuck it, might as well go out with a bang. I wonder why he's flying to London?"

"Umm?" Nick picked up a copy of National Geographic, flicked through it hastily then tucked it back inside the rack, fingering the edge of the cover.

"Are you alright? You've been quiet all morning."

"Me? I'm fine........Actually I'm not. Let's get a coffee"

They wandered over to Starbucks where Nick unburdened himself, hanging his head in shame. "Something strange happened last night. D'you know that cute waitress from the restaurant?"

"The one with the pretty face?"

"She was flirting with me, and I didn't do anything about it."

"Why not? She was nice her."

"That's what *I* want to know. There's more. You're not gonna believe this.....So I go back to my room, right, and I'm lying on the bed watching the match.........."

"The *match!?*"

"*Listen!.........*So I'm lying there and a knock comes at the door. I open it to find the most beautiful woman I've ever seen asking to use the bathroom."

"Really!*"*

"So.......so she walks in, takes all her clothes off and stands there naked, literally *begging* me to shag her............"

"You're *joking!*"

"I wish to God I were."

"What happened?"

"Nothing. I carried on watching the football."

Giles' bulbous eyes popped. *"What!?.......*But you *hate* football!!"

"I know. That's what worries me."

CHAPTER NINE

Midway between the Gherkin and the Shard lay the headquarters of Global Pharmaceuticals, a steel and glass monolith whose impenetrable aspect engendered in the passerby feelings of reverence and awe. What went on behind the sheer cliff face of those blacked out windows tapering up into the clouds? Who were the important looking men in grey suits arriving each morning in chauffeur-driven limousines, their faces as mysterious as their offshore bank accounts? Where was the usual corporate logo emblazoned across the entrance?

Strolling into reception Daniel knew he was entering the holy of holies. The very fabric of the building hummed with colossal deals and astonishing takeovers. Global Pharmaceuticals did exactly what it said on the tin; the bluest of blue chip companies whose ruthless practices had propelled it into the Forbes Top Ten, two places behind Royal Dutch Shell. Scourge of the environmental lobby, there wasn't an ecosystem they wouldn't desecrate or a family run business they wouldn't ruin in order to get what they wanted. Ruthlessness was their DNA. Daniel had admired them for years. He first read about them in the late 90's after they were taken to court by Greenpeace for trampling on the rights of the Tonami people, an endangered tribe living in the Indonesian rainforest. Keepers of lost secrets, they were rumoured to know the whereabouts of a mythical plant believed to slow down the ageing process. But instead of negotiating with the tribe, respecting their cultural sensibilities, Global Pharmaceuticals had whisked the chief off to a five star hotel in Singapore, plying him with cocaine and prostitutes. Daniel followed the trial for weeks, secretly rooting for 'GP', as he called them. Bliss it was on that morning when his father stormed into his office, threw down a copy of the *Financial Times* in disgust and said, "Those gangsters have got off on a technicality!" From then on Daniel followed their progress through the pages of the *FT,* dazzled by their brutal business methods and astonishing greed. That's why, on landing at Heathrow three days ago, he'd contacted JP Merrick -- the sixty year old CEO -- to arrange a meeting. Certain of success he'd booked a suite at the Dorchester. No way he was going to offer chamcha to a tin pot company like Page Pharmaceuticals. His father would only shake his head and say, "Absolutely not! Messing around with Nature like that! It's totally unethical!" Unlike JP Merrick, who was listening to his story with childlike rapture. "Incredible! What's the name of this tribe you say?" He spoke with a soft public school accent, his swarthy complexion and dark eyes swimming with possibilities.

"I didn't." Daniel couldn't believe JP's ruthlessness, trying to wheedle out the tribe's name so he could send his own people into the rainforest and swindle him out of his discovery. Nevertheless he admired a man who could stoop so low. I'm playing with the big boys now!

JP Merrick nodded his head respectfully. He recognised his mirror image, both men capable of selling their own grandmothers. Rising from his desk he strode up and down his carpeted office. It was furnished with Picassos and Louis XV antiques, its massive plate glass window overlooking the Thames. "Well, if what you say about this little plant is true, then you can write your own cheque."

"I intend to. Plus stock options."

"I wouldn't expect anything less, Daniel. I look forward to your presentation to the board."

"I'll need a couple of days to prepare."

"Shall we say Friday? Ten thirty?"

"Great.......Oh! You don't have any women on the board do you? Only they might get upset."

JP Merrick was astonished. "Good God, no! Who do you think we are, the BBC! As far as I'm concerned a woman's place is in the kitchen!"

"You sound like you don't need the drug, Mr Merrick."

"Let's just say I run a tight ship at home.........Well, see you on Friday." They shook hands. "One thing puzzles me. Why aren't you pursuing this with your father's company?"

"Page Pharmaceuticals! Do me a favour! They're far too small to take on such a massive project. Anyway, I've already emailed my resignation."

"You believe in it *that* much, do you?"

"Absolutely."

JP Merrick looked at Daniel with paternal devotion -- his own son Edmond had left home years ago and was currently wasting his life working as a Human Rights lawyer in Strasburg, seduced there by a fiery French journalist who'd put all sorts of radical ideas into his head. In a rare moment never before witnessed by his wife or closest friends -- especially not his wife -- JP Merrick slipped his corporate mask and dared to reveal his true feelings. "The bitches have got it coming!"

* * *

When Charles Page read Daniel's email he felt sick to the stomach. First there was Nick's damning report into his behaviour during the ill fated expedition, and now, three days later, this. He reread the email, certain cruel phrases catching his eye -- *'You never supported me!' 'My brilliant ideas!' 'That cocksucker Slater!' 'No wonder mum left!'* -- ending with a bizarre reference to *'the Nobel Prize for Chemistry!!!!!'* For years he'd realised his son was a wastrel, a good time Charlie fit for nothing but the tanning salon and the shallow charms of the sports car showroom. As a father he'd given him everything a son could wish for; encouraging him to join the family business, fast tracking him up the corporate ladder. But he always knew, from the moment Daniel set fire to his tree house, that things would end badly. Only a cold hard hearted liar could possibly blame the poor unfortunates off the council estate. Didn't he realise, standing there spouting his cock-and-bull story, that his clothes reeked of petrol? Perhaps Daniel was right. Maybe things would have turned out differently if his mother had stayed. I should have stood up for myself, thought Charles. Shown some backbone. But I loved her so much I just wanted to please her.

From the lab window Nick contemplated a truly wonderful sight -- Daniel's vacant parking space. Three days it had lain empty. Never had a slice of tarmac looked so good. There was no way back for the spoilt bastard now. But despite his smugness he still couldn't rid himself of the awful memory of his last night in Rio. Again and again he replayed her astonishing entrance; the spine tingling brush of her fingers, her soft sexy voice and blatant invitation to "Pour us both a drink while I use the bathroom." And then, oh then, her erotic sashay through the humid air, the crackle of her stockings, her hair let loose like a golden storm, the awe consuming sight as she peeled off her dress to reveal a body so mesmerising sparks flew in his brain. "Fuck me.".......Fuck me; was ever a more beautiful phrase uttered in the English language. So beautiful it eluded Shakespeare.

* * *

Daniel dug his fork into a crisp rasher of bacon, sliced it with his knife and dunked it into the soft heart of his poached egg, puncturing its delicate membrane. A tsunami of yellow liquid oozed across the plate, enveloping the fanlike edges of his organic field mushrooms. He'd stayed at the Dorchester many times of course, but never had his breakfast tasted so good. Not even after he'd bedded a TOWIE starlet he'd met the previous night in *Boujis.* If the viewers could have seen the tricks she turned!

He sipped his coffee, glancing at the clock on the wall. 8.30am. Two hours to go before the board meeting at Global Pharmaceuticals. For the past two days he'd been ensconced in his suite working on the presentation; refining his slick patter, polishing each sentence so that it glowed with a Byzantine like brilliance. Reading through his notes one last time he realised it was more than just a sales pitch, it was a comprehensive and detailed explanation into the inner workings of the female sex; the tricks of the trade so to speak. One final piece of the jigsaw was missing -- a name for the new wonder drug. He could hardly call it chamcha. He needed something snappy, something that would excite the male population. He first thought about calling it 'Revenge', but discounted that -- too aggressive. Then it came to him; Nick had used the exact same word the night he rejected the sexual advances of the high class hooker, a word so powerful it had blazed across the banners of the oppressed for centuries........'Freedom.'

He took the lift to his suite on the fifth floor and changed into a charcoal black Gieves & Hawkes classic pinstripe, white shirt and cornflower blue tie. Looking in the mirror he congratulated himself on his choice of tie -- the splash of colour would add a touch of rainforest splendour to the sombre boardroom. On his last visit to Global Pharmaceuticals he noticed that JP Merrick had a pretty blonde secretary, so before leaving the Dorchester he ate a root of chamcha. Nothing must deflect him from his path.

With an hour to kill before the presentation he took himself off to the nearest Ferrari showroom. There, on a slowly revolving platform, was the gorgeously proportioned Le Ferrari, a gleaming red mistress who would do as she was told and never answer back.

117

"How much?" asked Daniel.

"One million pounds, sir."

"I'll take it."

He was about to complete the paperwork when the chamcha kicked in. He dropped the pen and thought, What am I doing? I don't need this car. Not anymore.

Fearing for his bonus the hovering salesman enquired, "Is everything alright, sir?"

Daniel stood up, leaving the paperwork unsigned. "I'd get another job if I were you."

"Beg your pardon, sir."

He gestured towards a line of pillar-box red Ferraris. "They're going the way of the dinosaurs."

He walked outside and jumped into a taxi. Driving through Chelsea a forest of For Sale signs outside a swanky apartment block caught his eye. He made a mental note of the estate agent. His life in Wilmslow was over. He needed a resurrection pad grand enough to reflect his soon-to-be-confirmed status as the man who defeated women. Many had tried, from Julius Cesar to Henry VIII, but all had been undone by that poisonous seed planted at birth by Mother Nature.......lust. Armies would never conquer it, neither would the wisdom of philosophers. Only he, Daniel Page, had found the one true cure that would propel mankind into a glorious, stress free future. Surely now, without the maddening distraction of the female form, man could achieve anything. Take cancer. For too long pretty lab assistants in tight white coats and big sexy glasses had befuddled the brains of eminent professors who, instead of peering into their microscopes, fantasised about taking them away for the weekend. Then there was global agreement on climate change. How could anyone solve that when you had all those cute interpreters whispering into minister's ears? And it was only a matter of time before a fight broke out on the International Space Station over some doe-eyed cosmonatrix, sending it crashing to Earth. Women in Space! They were asking for trouble! No, when chamcha hit the streets it would leave men free to concentrate on the important things in life, like liberty and the pursuit of happiness; real happiness that didn't depend on the whims of a woman. Of course there would be casualties -- sports car manufacturers, luxury watches, designer labels, men's grooming products. All would become extinct as the male sex reverted to its more natural, slovenly state. Jewellers and florists would be hit hard. So would Michelin star restaurants and travel agents peddling romantic weekends away for two. Paris would become a ghost town, tumbleweed blowing along the Champs Elysees. Apart from off licenses there wasn't a shop on the high street that was safe. A whole new way of living was called for, this time slanted towards men. There would be no more trailing round the shops on a Saturday looking at carpets and curtains. No more bank holidays ruined by wild goose chases to DIY stores. As for garden centres, forget it!

A schism of the profoundest kind rippled through the universe. Whole galaxies shook. On the deepest subatomic level elementary particles like quarks and gluons transmitted panic stricken messages along invisible binary systems. Sitting at her desk on the fourth floor of Crown House in Wilmslow, HQ of a data processing company, Sophie experienced a sudden pang of longing. Out of the blue Daniel came into her mind. She hadn't thought about him for weeks. Ever since the company bash he had bombarded her with hundreds of lovesick texts and heartfelt answer phone messages, begging her to take him back. Then, suddenly, inexplicable silence. She knew he was back in the country through a friend who worked at Page Pharmaceuticals. All sorts of stories were going round concerning his despicable behaviour in the rainforest -- his crass racist jokes, his animal cruelty, his descent into cannibalism, not to mention rumours of a Roman style orgy in his hotel room in Rio. Days on end it lasted, every prostitute in Copacabana used and abused. Drugs too! Oh yes, no stone had gone unturned in his rampant pursuit of pleasure. But guess what, that wimp Slater had humiliated him. Apparently they'd got into a fight over a steep gorge. Savage blows were traded. Daniel grabbed a knife but Slater was too quick for him. In an awesome display of King Fu, Slater had first disarmed him then sent him flying with a dazzling spin-kick to the head. But the best bit was that his father had disowned him and he was now destitute, living on the streets of the capital.

This final piece of news tugged Sophie's heartstrings. Deep down she was the maternal type. Yes Daniel was arrogant, yes he was spoilt, but surely now he'd learnt his lesson? She imagined him slumped in some doorway, full of regrets. His phone had obviously been stolen -- hence the radio silence. Even now he was calling out to her. Her man. Yes, *her* man! After all they'd never really broken up. It was her mother who'd kyboshed the relationship! She couldn't desert him now. Not in his hour of need. All her motherly instincts made her get up from her desk and rush outside. She took out her mobile and dialled his number.

Daniel paid the driver and was on his way into reception when his iPhone rang. He looked at the screen 'Soph.' Oh! She wants to talk now does she!

"Hello?"

"Hi, Danny. It....it's me........How are you?"

"What do *you* care?"

"Don't be like that.........Listen, I know you're in trouble.....Do you need money? If you do I can send you.........."

"What the fuck are you on about?"

"Come home. Let's sort things out......I miss you."

Without the chamcha her sweet velvety voice would have made him jump back in the taxi and head straight for Euston Station. He marvelled at the inherent gift women had for tearing open men's hearts with innocent words like 'home' and 'I miss you.' But he was immune to such sorcery.

"Sophie?"

"Yeah?"

"Go fuck yourself."

He took the lift to the thirtieth floor and strolled into the empty boardroom. As requested, a laptop linked to a large screen had been set up. He inserted a memory stick loaded with data and booted up the computer. Great truths were about to be told, so for dramatic effect he lowered the blinds so that the boardroom took on the atmosphere of a seer's cave. At 10.30 precisely the doors swung open. In filed twenty or so immaculately dressed executives, most of whom had flown in from various parts of the globe. Summoned to London by JP Merrick they were told to prepare themselves for the "presentation of a lifetime." There was Ping Yan Lou, head of the Chinese division, a tubby fifty year old with expressionless features and an icy demeanour. Married with three children, Mr Lou lived in a luxury mansion on the outskirts of Shanghai. A talented artist in his youth, he was forced by a domineering mother to give up the brush in favour of a business degree at Beijing University. When at last the old woman died and he got married, all he'd done was swap one despot for another. Not even a pencil was allowed into the house. That's why he loved travelling to Europe on business. He would lie to his wife beforehand, exaggerating the amount of time he had to be away. Once business was concluded he would catch the first available flight to Paris where, dressed in bohemian clothes like his hero Picasso, he would wander the streets of Montmartre with his sketch pad dreaming of a life devoted to art. Another board member was *Signor* Alessandro Fabretti. Head of the Italian division he lived in Rome with his third wife Elisabetta. A serial adulterer, he was forever having affairs with TV starlets and fashion models, sneaking them into his spectacular apartment overlooking the Vatican while his wife was having dinner with friends. It was almost as if he wanted to get caught, as he had done by his two previous wives. Marriage just didn't suit him. But he was petrified of his own company, emasculated by a childhood spent wrapped in cottonwool. The only boy among four elder sisters, his mother had doted on him, calling him the Prince and showering him with kisses. If only he had the courage to live as a bachelor. The women he could have!

JP Merrick was the last to enter. He had a quick word with Ping Yan Lou then addressed the rest of the board who had all taken their seats.

"Fellow board members. Welcome. You're probably wondering why I've called you here at such short notice. The fact is, an extraordinary discovery has been made. One that, if proved correct, will change the lives of every man on the planet. The profits from this particular drug will be huge, and I'm proud to say that its discoverer, Daniel Page, has chosen to offer it to Global Pharmaceuticals........So, gentlemen, sit back and prepare to be astonished."

Daniel got his feet. A murmur went round the boardroom. "Gentlemen. What chance have we got against this?" He pressed the Enter key on the laptop. Instead of the usual boring data illustrating the unstoppable rise of cancer, a huge full length photo of Kelly Brook wearing a bikini appeared on the screen. Instantly the room fell silent. Certain board members who were shuffling papers or glancing at their iPhones suddenly froze. Mouths gaping, they stared at the screen with gobstopper eyes. There were nervous coughs and "hems," followed by schoolboy smirks. Then, remembering where they were, fixed, serious expressions. Again Daniel hit the Enter key. This time a smouldering Mila Kunis in sequined lingerie popped up, pouting into camera. The men sat there like waxwork dummies, cancer long since forgotten. A succession of stunning scantily clad sirens followed -- Scarlett Johansson, Beyonce, Jessica Alba, Rihanna -- each women eliciting stifled moans and sharp intakes of breath. Daniel noticed *Signor* Fabretti in particular. He was sitting close to the screen, pulling at his shirt collar as though unable to breath. The images speeded up, one after the other, a litany of naked flesh and enchanting faces. Daniel began to speak, his voice booming like a Hollywood movie trailer......"Women. Ever since the dawn of time men have been obsessed with them. From the clothes we wear to the cars we drive, we've strutted around like peacocks for one reason and one reason only; to attract the female sex. And do they deserve such lavish attention? Not in my book. Women are *born* with beautiful bodies, they haven't actually done anything to *deserve* them! While we men have built cities and created empires. All that energy, all that passion! And for what? Just to impress the ladies. Don't believe me? Alright, ask yourself this; why do I work so hard? Why do I put up with so much bullshit when it comes to relationships?......The answer, gentlemen, couldn't be more simple; sex and the fear of loneliness......Let's start with sex."

He ran a video taken from a Channel 4 documentary about attraction. A tiny camera had been placed in the glasses of a thirty year old man, tracking the movement of his eyes as walked down a busy street. Every few seconds passing cleavages, thighs, faces and bottoms were zone in on. "Ring any bells, gentlemen?"

There was a clearing of throats and a few stilled titters.

"Like this poor shmuck they strapped a camera to we can't stop thinking about sex. How can we? We're programmed by Nature. From the moment our umbilical cord is cut, like sex-crazed salmon the quest is on to be reunited with a woman. And when the net finally closes, we all know what *that* means, don't we, gentlemen?........Correct; a 'relationship.'"

A collective groan rippled through the boardroom, Ping Yan Lou groaning louder than most.

Daniel stopped the video. "This is when a woman comes into her own and starts to take control. We're now a 'couple'. We're no longer ourselves but are part of a 'relationship'.........We have a relationship for what reason? Because we *want* to? Because it makes us *happy*? Don't kid yourself. We have a relationship because we're terrified of being on our own. But if we weren't so insecure in the first place we wouldn't *need* a relationship! And who's fault is *that,* eh?"

Signor Fabretti nodded enthusiastically.

"Now don't get me wrong, I'm not advocating a world without women. What I *am* advocating is, women on *our* terms."

Heads craned forward. Hopeful expressions shone.

"Think how happy we would be. Think of what we could achieve if we banished women from our minds. Imagine the possibilities!"

Ping Yan Lou saw himself in a studio in Montmartre, the brightly lit space crammed with canvases and tubes of paint. On a simple wooden table the remnants of last night's meal -- an empty bottle of wine and half eaten baguette. On a battered chaise a model he'd met in some disreputable cafe, his only thought to capture the effect of Parisian light streaming over her flaxen hair.

Signor Fabretti imagined a tranquil life of self indulgence, where the absence of women meant peace of mind instead of the usual stomach churning insecurities.

Perhaps then he could finally enjoy the wonderful view of the Eternal City from his balcony.

Daniel gilded the lily. "We could please ourselves what we do and when we do it. We could play golf when we want, watch football when we want....."

"And snooker!"

"........*And* snooker! without the constant fear of rejection. Because let's face it, fear is a women's number one weapon of choice. Remove fear, and they're powerless.....Well, gentlemen, imagine no more, because the miracle we've all been waiting for has finally arrived." He took from his pocket a bunch of chamcha roots, thrusting them aloft like the Olympic torch. "Behold! I have in my hand the answer to all our prayers. A miracle plant I discovered in the rainforest. This little plant not only suppresses our sexual desires, more importantly it controls our deepest and most profound need.......the need to be loved."

"But I *love* women!" pleaded Pavel Nozdryov, standing in for the head of the Russian division who was unable to attend due to marriage problems.

Daniel smirked. "Don't we all."

"Then why would I want to banish them?"

"You won't. You'll be attracting them."

"How?"

"Because women always want what they can't have."

"I can testify to that!" said a stressed out executive -- *Monsieur* Henri Pascal, head of the French division, a father of two with a particular demanding mistress. Only last night he'd visited her cosy apartment in the 7th *Arrondissment*. The sex was amazing, disgusting acts punctuated with birdlike calls in his ear. "When are you leaving your wife?" "Oh Henri I adore you." "Think of it, you can have me every night."

"That's the beauty of this new wonder drug," continued Daniel. "You regulate the dose to suit yourself.

For instance, how many of us start the day with a list of things we want to do, only to get sidetracked by a pretty face? It might be a gorgeous waitress or a woman with amazing breasts. Common sense goes out of the window. We're like dogs on heat, unable to think straight. It's not as if we *want* to feel like that, our bodies *force* us to! But what this drug does, it allows us to ignore those signals and carry on with our day, free from sexual frustration. Now that's gotta be a good thing. Can you imagine the effect this is gonna have on women? For thousands of years we've lusted after them, lay at their feet and worshipped them. And they love it. They've come to expect it! It's given them power. You think you know what power is, don't you, gentlemen, with your fancy jobs and your corporate jets? Step into a woman's body for a day, that's *real* power. Why do you think they spend so long pampering themselves? It sure as hell ain't for the poor shmuck they live with! They do it for the attention, for the sheer joy of being wanted. It's part of their self worth. It's what makes them tick. Deny them that and they'll be eating out of our hands. I'm talking about the Holy Grail -- sex on our own terms."

The room exploded "HOW? HOW? TELL US! PLEASE!!!"

"Simple; all we do is, we take the drug, enjoy ourselves to the max, then, when we're ready to have sex, we stop taking it. But here's the clever bit; because we'll all be on the drug at different times, there'll *always* be a regular supply of women, just gagging for it. We'll all be flavour of the month, twenty four seven three six five! Ugly men, fat men, yes, even *bald* men! Because let's face it, there's nothing a woman wouldn't do to get what she wants....... and that *includes* being nice!"

"If only!" exclaimed Sheik Azzan Bin Mohamed, head of the Middle East division, a handsome forty year old resplendent in his flowing white robes. "I have many wives. None of them do as I ask. And they are surly. It is most frustrating!"

Daniel smashed the table with his fist. "Why do we put up with it, eh? Why? We try our best! We bend over backwards to please them! But nothing is ever good enough! Moan, moan, moan, that's the only thanks we get! I don't know about you but I've had enough! It's time we took control of our lives! It's time we threw off the shackles that have imprisoned us for centuries!.........Gentlemen, it's time for 'FREEDOM!'"

"HERE! HERE!" The room burst into spontaneous applause. Never had a presentation gone down so well, not even when Viagra was first mooted. There was clapping and cheering as each board member contemplated the effect of the drug on his own private life. Ping Yan Lou, normally so reserved, hugged *Signor* Fabretti, who in turn patted the back of a beaming Henri Pascal. But it was left to Sheik Azzan Bin Mohamed to capture the mood. Thinking of that awful moment each morning before he entered his harem, he set up a clarion call that was instantly taken up by the rest of the board. "No more fear!....No...more...fear!......NO MORE FEAR!!"

CHAPTER TEN

A delighted JP Merrick took Daniel's arm and led him out of the boardroom down the corridor towards his office. On the way he past his pretty blonde secretary who for years had teased him with a succession of short skirts and low-cut blouses. It surprised her that, instead of the usual simpering smile or lustful stare, he looked at her with the cynical amusement of a big game hunter about to wipe out an endangered species.

Entering his office JP Merrick clapped his hands. "Marvellous presentation, Daniel! First class! You had the board eating out of your hand." Unable to keep still he walked over to the window and stared out over the capital. "You do realise this drug of ours will change the world!"

"Ours?"

"*Yours,* of course, until you sign the rights over to Global Pharmaceuticals. Which, as I said, you can name your own price. Before that we need to start a series of clinical trials at our facility in Suffolk. Rigorous trails you understand?"

"Do as many as you like."

"Just one thing. Once the drug's been manufactured and put on sale to the general public, what's to stop women taking it?"

"It doesn't work on women. Makes them sick."

"Excellent!" JP Merrick scratched his head and proffered a shy grin. "Er....before you go, can I ask you a favour?"

"Shoot."

"It's erm, it's rather embarrassing.....My erm....my marriage isn't what it was....All that guff I gave you about running a tight ship.......it was er.....it was all bravado I'm afraid. The fact is my marriage hit the rocks years ago........So I was wondering if I could possibly.......Just a small amount you understand."

"Be my guest!" Daniel reached into his pocket and took out a root of chamcha. Before handing it over he looked JP Merrick in the eye. "Er.... I *have* taken out a patent."

"Goodness me! You don't think I would.........."

"So long as we know where we stand."

"Absolutely!"

"Good.......Take it ten minutes before you get home. The drug lasts about twenty four hours."

"Excellent!"

"And by the way, I've decided to call it 'Freedom'.

JP Merrick shook his head in admiration. "'Freedom'. Couldn't have put it better myself."

Sitting in the back seat of his chauffer driven Mercedes skimming through the Berkshire countryside, JP Merrick's thoughts drifted back to happier times. He recalled the day, some thirty years ago now, when he first brought his fiancée Barbara to visit the family home, Oldthorpe Manor, a magnificent country estate set in three thousand acres. Like Charles Ryder in Brideshead Revisited, the moment she set eyes on the place she was besotted. Coming from a middle class background she had always dreamed of marrying into a titled family. They had met at a dinner party in Chelsea thrown by one of JP's banker friends. Barbara worked as a PA at the time for the chairman of Sotheby's; access to certain rich clients propelling her up the social ladder. Determined to make the most of her situation she stalked the dinner party circuit on the lookout for a wealthy husband. So when she came across JP Merrick, boasting about how one day he would inherit Oldthorpe Manor, she began a campaign to capture his wallet. It was brilliantly conceived and superbly executed. Sitting opposite him she first observed his massive ego, his childlike need to be the centre of attention. So she praised and flattered him. She laughed at his jokes, mirroring not only his body language but his

Right-wing views. She even feigned an interest in his passion for fox hunting. As a secret animal rights supporter this was the most difficult thing of all. But the moment she saw Oldthorpe Manor, any sympathy for the fox went right out of the window. Well, they *were* vermin after all. And thinking about it, how could animals possibly have 'rights'! The whole idea was ridiculous! Drifting through the sumptuous state apartments, a shy and sensitive wall flower besotted with her beau, gentle, kind and attentive, she stole the hearts of the Merrick family. Everyone, that is, apart from JP's mother, the formidable Lady Catherine. The instant Barbara entered the Great Hall, with her sweet, modest demeanour, Catherine knew she was a gold digger. She knew because thirty years ago she had played the exact same role. And like her grotesque mother-in-law before her she vowed never to let the middle class slut anywhere near her son's heart. So at dinner she treated Barbara with cruel indifference; glaring at her during the six course banquet, hunting for *faux pas*. "Oh look, JP! She's picked up the wrong fork!......*Silly* girl!" But all this did, as it had done with Catherine's mother-in-law, was to make her son pursue her all the more. Despite the rows, the late night phone calls threatening to disinherit him, Catherine finally admitted defeat, undone by a stratagem she herself had once deployed. During the wedding ceremony, such was her hatred of Barbara she resorted to wearing earplugs to avoid hearing the vows. But when the moment came to say "I do," Barbara glanced over her shoulder and stared at Catherine in triumph.

The marriage began well enough. A month after the wedding Lady Catherine died in a road accident along with JP's father, so the couple left their draughty cottage on the estate and moved into Oldthorpe Manor. A year later she gave birth to their only son, a sickly child named Edmond. But inevitably, like most marriages, it wasn't long before boredom set in. She no longer laughed at his jokes, fetched him his slippers or pecked him on the cheek before he set off for the City each morning; little things that make men happy. In fact the very sight of him got on her nerves. So did his constant need for attention. So did the endless rolling acres she could see from every window in the house. She was a city girl for heaven's sake! Why had she buried herself in the country miles away from her friends; friends who never came to visit, certain of having their noses rubbed in it. It was alright for JP, he was happy enough with his tedious job and his stupid fox hunting! What pleasure did *she* have, apart from bullying the servants and strutting round the village? But of course she would never admit she was bored. Hadn't she schemed and plotted for just such a life? To admit as much would reveal her as a fool, no better than the shallow social climbers she often encountered at hunt balls. So like most women down the ages she took her frustration out on her husband, starting with disparaging remarks in the bedroom concerning his love making. She was sick of the same old routine -- two minutes fingering, a quick lick between the legs and then over onto one's back. "For heaven's sake, JP! Try something different!"

"Alright. How about sucking me off?"

"No I will not! Disgusting!"

"You used to."

"That was before we were married! We're decent people now!"

Poor JP. It wasn't long before he was reduced to using the services of high class call girls at five hundred pounds a pop. When denying him sex no longer bothered him, she moved on to the very core of his being -- fox hunting and the memory of his dear mother. It was a two pronged attack, ruthlessly executed. First she banned the Oldthorpe Hunt from meeting in front of the house. JP pleaded with her, appealing to her sense of tradition. "But darling, the hunt's gathered here for centuries. It's part of our history."

Barbara was unmoved "I don't give a *damn!* I'm sick of being woken up by stupid bugle calls and dogs barking! Not to mention those *bloody* women with their *obnoxious* voices! No, JP! I've made up my mind!"

"Very well, dear. We'll meet in the village."

"And another thing, what kind of a person chases a poor fox around the countryside? It's *damned* cruel if you ask me!"

"But........but don't you remember, you used to enjoy coming out on the hunt."

"Only to get away from your mother! She humiliated me! She went out of her way to make my life a misery! She never wanted me to marry you, you know!"

"Nonsense."

"It's not nonsense! From day one she made it plain I wasn't good enough! Bloody snob!"

"Steady on Barbara!"

"No, JP! You weren't privy to half the things that went on! Oh I can tell you a thing or two about that woman. I've dug into her background. It's says in Who's Who she's descended from the Earls of Warwick. Liar! Her father was an accountant from Solihull!"

"Nothing wrong with that, dear. Your father was an accountant."

One thing Barbara couldn't stand was being reminded of her own middle class upbringing. "Right! That's it! I've been meaning to do this for a long time!" She rushed over to the fireplace and wrenched from the wall a portrait of Lady Catherine dressed in hunt clothes and brandishing a whip.

"What are you doing?"

"Something I should have done a long time ago!" She raised the picture above her head. "Always criticising! Always judging!"

"Barbara! No! Put the picture down! Please!"

Eyes blazing she slammed it against the corner of a table, tearing the canvas.

"Oh God! Barbara!"

She hurled it onto the fire, adding, with a Hollywood flourish. "Now you know how Rebecca felt when she first came to Mandalay!"

It took a long time for JP to forgive her, but forgive her he did, though oddly she was the one who didn't speak to him. He coaxed her out of silence by resigning from the Oldthorpe Hunt and removing every last photograph of his mother. Things improved for a while. During fox hunting season Barbara took great pleasure in watching JP's reaction as the distant sound of the hunting horn echoed through the valley. Sitting in his chair by the fire reading the *Financial Times* he would gaze longingly through the window, transported back to a magical world of mud splattered fields and galloping horses. Barbara indulged him for a second or two before delivering a sharp schoolmistressy cough. Jolted out of his reverie, JP glanced over at her, a guilty look on his face. Barbara stared at him ferociously. He cleared his throat, shook the newspaper and went back to his article. A thin smile curled her top lip. But it wasn't long before the ranting started again. Anything could set her off -- the servants, the weather, even the way the curtains hung. The second his key went in the door she was at his throat.

But the worst moment of their marriage came fifteen years later, on their son's twenty second birthday. Edmond had graduated from Oxford with a third class law degree. He'd just completed a year's internship at a barrister's chambers owned by a chum of JP's. It was there he had fallen under the spell of a radical left wing journalist from Lille named Fernande. A tigerish brunette with cropped hair, she worked for *Le Figaro* and had been sent over to London to write a series of articles about the corrupting influence of money. Edmond bumped into her one night at a fashionable art gallery in Shoreditch. Dressed in tight black leggings and a lime green puffer jacket, she was standing on her own examining a set of Tracy Emin canvases. There was something about the little tomboy that fascinated him. Despite her size she exuded an inner strength. He'd always been attracted to strong women. He watched her intently, the way she shook her head disparagingly at each artwork. At one point a pretentious couple walked past waxing lyrical about how the paintings 'said something' about the artist's tortured soul. Fernande spluttered into her glass of red. "Bulle...shit!"

That was it. Edmond was in love. He somehow managed to pluck up the courage to talk to her. They left the gallery and took a cab to Soho. After a delicious plate of oysters and a chilled bottle of *Montrachet* they went for a midnight stroll along the Embankment. Fernande spoke passionately about her childhood. Born to working class parents on a tough housing estate on the outskirts of Lille, life was a constant struggle. At college she'd flirted with lesbianism before dedicating herself to left wing politics. Edmond nodded as she poured forth her vitriol on the capitalist system. Passing the Houses of Parliament, its floodlit reflection shimmering in the waters of the Thames, she pointed at it and said, in her cute but severe French accent "I would like to tear down every last stone of that rotten building!"

Deep inside Edmond felt something stir. "I know what you mean. Hateful, hateful!"

They began an affair, which consisted of Edmond running her around London in his Jag and paying for everything. It wasn't long before she moved in to his basement flat in Belgravia. "Perfect," she said, "to study the decadent practises of the upper class."

Soon Barbara became suspicious of the bolshie French voice that sometimes answered the phone on a Sunday evening. Eventually she got Edmond to admit he'd met someone special; though he didn't go into much detail about her family or social connections.

Who was this mysterious Frenchwomen? And what were the consequences for the Merrick dynasty? "It's your birthday in a fortnight," exclaimed Barbara, when her son was being suspiciously evasive. "Bring her to Oldthorpe for the weekend! I'm *dying* to meet her."

"But Mother, we were planning on......"

"I won't hear another word, Edmond!"

"Yes, Mother."

For two weeks leading up to the visit Edmond hardly slept. To soften the blow he took Fernande out for dinner at *La Garvroche* and told her about his family's privileged ancestry, their enormous wealth and vast country estate.

It came as a shock to her left wing sensibilities. "I knew they were rich, but not *that* rich! Why did you lie to me?"

"Darling! I didn't lie! It just didn't seem important."

The touchy elf became all haughty. "On no, it wouldn't! Money never does to those who have it! Typical!" The memory of her own mother rose up in her mind, the painful fact she used to clean for a wealthy family in an upmarket suburb of Lille. "And you are sole heir to this disgusting fortune?"

"Yes," he replied sheepishly. "But it's not something I'm proud of."

"I wouldn't be in a relationship with you if you were!........You have no brothers or sisters, you say?"

"No. I'm an only child."

"You are sure?"

"Positive."

"No illegitimate siblings waiting in the wings?"

"No."

"So it will all to come to you eventually?"

"Yes."He leaned across the table and slipped his hand into hers. "Look, Fernande, if you'd rather not go......"

"Oh I'm going alright! I want to see for myself this privileged world of yours!"

The weekend was a disaster. Barbara expected an obsequious gold digger, all wide eyed and modest, taking in every last detail of the house while at the same time dreaming of becoming its chatelaine, as she herself had done. Fernande was the complete opposite. Oldthorpe barely registered. In fact when Edmond brought her into the Great Hall, explaining the house's history and pointing out various family portraits, she began to yawn. Barbara couldn't *believe* what the slut was wearing -- ripped jeans, Charlie Ebdo T-shirt and cherry red Doc Martins. The way she chewed gum disgusted her. So did her politics. And her revolting table manners!!!!

But the worst moment came when the servants were clearing away the dinner plates. Despite Edmond pleading with her on the drive up not to mention it, Fernande took great pleasure in proclaiming, "Edmond and I are moving to Strasbourg. He's got a job as a Human Rights lawyer for Amnesty."

Barbara waited until Fernande had gone to bed before confronting Edmond on the stairs. "Listen to me! If you even *think* about moving abroad with that creature, you can kiss goodbye to your inheritance. You'll be penniless, do you understand?"

It was the hardest thing Edmond had ever done. He looked at his mother and said, "I don't care. I love her." He turned his back and walked up the stairs.

Barbara burst into JP's bedroom screaming, "This is all your fault!"

"How is it *my* fault?"

"You men! You're all *weak*!!"

Edmond and Fernande left early the next morning without saying goodbye. Lying in bed running over the previous day's events, Barbara couldn't believe Fernande hadn't wanted what she had wanted. Then it came to her, the bitch's ingenious plan. Of course! Edmond had obviously told her about the numerous girls he'd brought to Oldthorpe in the past -- how well behaved they were, how they had thrown themselves at him and done everything to please him. Typical spoilt brat he soon got bored and given them the heave-ho. So instead of trying to ingratiate herself, Fernande had gone out of her way to drive a wedge between the family. It's either them or me! And the more radical and couldn't care less she appeared about money, the more Edmond fell in love with her. But this was the clever part; deep down Fernande knew there was no way JP would disinherit his only son. And so it was only a matter of time before she returned to Oldthorpe in triumph, mistress of the manor. Barbara bit down hard on her bottom lip. The little French whore had outfoxed her.

JP saw the sign for Oldthorpe. In fifteen minutes he'd be home. Oh God! He took the chamcha root Daniel had given him, broke it into bite size pieces and popped them into his mouth. The taste took him back to childhood; to the liquorish sticks he used to chew in the playground at prep school. Life was carefree back then. Strange, but the same blissful feeling began to seep into his system. Going home no longer bothered him. He felt elated, as though he'd just received news of his wife's death. Yes, that's exactly how it felt. Barbara was dead to him! Driving through the village he saw a sign chalked up outside the pub -- HUNT MEETING TONIGHT. 7PM. He knew what it was about. An ex hunting pal had told him a secret vote was taking place to decide whether or not to defy the ban; to pretend to go drag hunting but in reality chase their furry friends to the gates of hell. I'm damned well going to that! he said to himself. Already he was galloping across the fields on his favourite mare, clattering through bushes and leaping ditches to the wonderful baying of the hounds. Hunting was in his blood. Why had he let some obnoxious woman deny him his birthright? Well, those days are over. Then he remembered Barbara was throwing a dinner party for the vicar and his wife, an insipid couple who had nothing to say for themselves. Now *there* was a man under the thumb. He was more afraid of his wife than he was of God! No thank you, thought JP. I'll give that a miss.

Soon the wonderful stately pile loomed into view. There it was, shinning in the evening sun. What a magnificent house. The Merrick's had lived there for over seven hundred years. His heart sang as he travelled down the broad avenue of limes, the lake in the far distance gleaming like a mirror. He remembered going boating on it as a child. And the woods on the left! He shot his first rabbit in there! Shooting was another of his passions Barbara had put a stop to it. I must visit the gunroom tonight, thought JP. Give my favourite twelve bore a clean. Oldthorpe called to him like a long lost lover. For years her charms had been buried under a pall of gloom. A house like that should be enjoyed, not fussed over; a place where groundbreaking ideas could be discussed without a constant stream of sarcasm; a place that rang to music of the hounds. It suddenly came to him how lucky he was to have been born into such a privileged family -- inheriting a great estate, all the money he could wish for -- and vowed to make the most of it.

Whistling a Bach cantata he got out of the car and crunched across the gravel. He hadn't noticed it before, the swathe of acanthus leaves running the whole length of the portico, just below the Corinthian pediment. Quite charming. And look! There were bunches of grapes too, along with rows of tumbling cherubs. The house was a mishmash of styles -- part medieval, part Tudor, part neo classical -- with bits added here and there, like the huge Victorian conservatory and an Art Deco wing built in the 1920's. Taking revenge on her hated mother-in-law, down the centuries each successive chatelaine had changed the look of the house. The last great upheaval came in the 1960's when JP's mother badgered her husband into commissioning Swiss architect Le Corbusier to build a concrete extension onto the Art Deco wing. No sooner had Lady Catherine been laid to rest than Barbara added a mock medieval gable onto the Brutalist monstrosity. And so it went on, generation after generation. Gradually the house was becoming a pastiche, ruined by a series of bad tempered Pyrrhic victories. Driving around Oldthorpe each successive heir would gaze wistfully at the quaint cottages inhabited by estate workers, envious of their simple, stress free lifestyles. But inside these modest dwellings a domestic arms race was taking place, where hard pressed farmers, gamekeepers and grooms were browbeaten into purchasing the latest pickling jars, must have bellows and state-of-the-art clockwork spits.

JP had barely opened the front door before Barbara confronted him in the Great Hall. "Do stop *whistling* JP!" She was holding her cat, a loathsome tabby she smothered with affection.

He breezed past them. "Such a lovely evening I thought I'd go to the pub."

"You *are* joking!"

"Not in the least."

"We've got *guests* in an hour, *stupid!*"

He gambolled up the stairs, got changed and came back down. He found Barbara in the dining room fussing over the silver. "I'm off. Don't wait up."

She charged after him. "What the *hell* are you talking about! I've just *told* you, we've got *guests!*"

"And *I* told *you* I was going to the pub! Are you deaf, woman?"

"*WHAT!!!!* Now just you listen to me....."

"No! You listen to me! They're your friends, not mine. And a boring lot they are too. Bye."

"Walk out that door JP and I won't be here when you get back!"

"Good! Go on then, out! And take that *bloody* cat with you!"

CHAPTER ELEVEN

The Global Pharmaceuticals Research Facility was hidden deep in the Suffolk countryside. Formally owned by the Ministry of Defence, it lay behind a parameter wall topped with razor wire. The company had bought the site a decade ago and transformed the odd assortment of buildings into a mini industrial estate of pristine white laboratories and secret animal testing stations. It was so hush-hush the locals had to invent their own bizarre theories -- a race of genetically altered humanoids was being developed; a drug that triples the intellectual capacity of the brain; a serum guaranteed to bring everlasting life. The truth was, they were right. Over the years things had gone on behind those walls that defied logic and caused villagers to bolt their doors when the sun went down. A huge three headed rat had once been glimpsed; strange flashing lights and terrible screams witnessed. Just to drive past the place gave the locals goose bumps.

Daniel pulled up at the entrance and gave his name to the security guard. Dressed in a black uniform with GP epaulettes, the guard returned to the gatehouse and picked up the phone, all the while keeping his eye on Daniel's car. A nodding of the head was seen before the security barrier was lifted and he was waved through. He drove along a twisting tree lined road flanked by strange windowless buildings. Men in white coats suddenly appeared, chatted for a few moments then vanished into an underground bunker.

Walking into reception he gave his name and was told to take a seat by a trickling fountain. He picked up the company magazine, casually flicking through its glossy pages. He came across an article on Ping Yan Lou opening a new research facility in Shanghai. Daniel recognised the same deadpan expression from the presentation two weeks ago. There he was, shaking hands with the Chairman of the Chinese Communist Party.

"Mr Page?"

A tall middle aged man with thin features wearing a light blue suit and bow tie appeared. Daniel stood up. "Daniel, please."

The man thrust out his hand. "Professor Jameson: head of clinical trials. Nice to meet you Daniel. If you'd like to come to my office." The professor escorted him down a brightly lit corridor. "This new drug of yours -- Freedom I believe it's called. I've never come across anything like it. Enormous potential. Absolutely enormous.....Freedom, eh? I'm *very* excited!"

"You're married then."

"How do you..........? Oh, yes, quite!"

"It's gonna change the world, Professor."

"Hopefully. That's what we're here to find out......Do come in.......Have a seat.......Now, we've gathered together a group of volunteers; students from our training programme -- male, heterosexual, just as you asked. As with all clinical trials one of them will be taking a placebo."

"Naturally."

"We've devised a series of rigorous tests to prove categorically whether or not the drug works."

"Oh it works alright," chuckled Daniel.

"Each of the student's vital signs will be individually monitored -- heart rate, blood pressure, that sort of thing -- to make sure no one cheats. Plus they've all abstained from sex for the past week....... including masturbation."

"Wow. When you said the tests were rigorous you weren't lying."

"Precisely...... Believe me, Daniel, what these students are about to go through no man on earth could possibly resist. Let's go and meet them."

Professor Jameson drove Daniel to a secluded building at the edge of the facility, close to where the giant mutant rat was glimpsed. Inside was a succession of locked rooms and security clearance doorways. Punching in a six digit code the professor opened a vacuum sealed door that led to a network of underground corridors.

"The students have no idea what this is about," explained the professor. "We've told them we're testing a new form of Viagra."

"The old double bluff, eh? Whose idea was that?"

"JP Merrick's."

"The crafty sod ."

"I can see his point. They'll be expecting to feel sexually aroused. It'll be interesting to see how they cope with the disappointment."

Daniel grinned. "They'll have to get used to that when they're married."

"Quite."

"How is JP, by the way?"

Approaching yet another sealed door Professor Jameson suddenly turned pale. "You've not heard, then?"

"Heard what?"

"Apparently he kicked his wife out two weeks ago. A real dragon by all accounts. The strange thing is, twenty four hours later he broke down in front of his secretary, telling her he'd made a terrible mistake and begging her to ring his wife to ask her to come home."

"What happened?"

"What do you think? The dragon moved straight back in. According to his secretary she's making his life a misery."

Daniel shook his head. "Men! The sooner we get Freedom on the market the better."

"I had JP on the phone this morning you know. You should have heard him! 'I don't care how much it costs! Freedom is to be given top priority!'"

143

"With a wife like that I'm not surprised!"

Thinking about his own wife, Professor Jameson grabbed Daniel's arm in desperation, pleading, "This drug it......it will work?"

"Course it'll work."

"It *must* work!"

"Professor.........Professor!"

"Umm?"

"You're hurting my arm."

"Oh! Sorry!" He punched in the code and took Daniel into a room equipped with computers and staffed by four white coated technicians. "As per your suggestion all the staff working on the tests are men."

"Good. The last thing we want is a women poking her nose in."

"Couldn't agree more. Keep our powder dry."

Through a one-way mirror Daniel could see six male students relaxing on comfortable armchairs reading a selection of magazines specially chosen for the test. In one pile were several copies of Penthouse, Playboy and Nuts, plus a body building magazine called Muscle. In the second, Famer's Weekly, The Caravaner, Practical Model Railways.

"Unsurprisingly the students are all reading girlie magazines," noted the professor. "Apart from the gay one."

"The gay one?"

"Oh yes, I forgot to mention; JP insisted we include a homosexual in the trail, in case there's a market for Freedom in the gay community.........Look, he's reading Muscle. Can you see? The burly chap on the front cover's obviously caught his attention."

"Obviously!"

Professor Jameson rolled his eyes. "Now they're all 'in the mood', I think it's time we started the test." He turned to one of the technicians. "Give the students their first dose of Freedom."

Hearing this his colleagues glanced at one another excitedly. There was something mystical about the word. It put hope into men's souls. Daniel congratulated himself on giving the product such a superb name. The technician picked up a tray of washed chamcha roots.

"One root each."

"Yes, professor." He left the room and reappeared a few moments later on the other side of the glass. The students took no notice of him; they were busy showing each other the various centrefolds.

The professor's voice boomed through speakers. "We're starting the trial now. Please take what you're given and carry on reading the magazines."

The technician handed each student a single root of chamcha and left the room. Without taking their eyes off the naked women the students began crunching and chewing.

Professor Jameson pointed at a computer screen. "Note the volunteer's heart rates."

"They've increased twofold since they started reading the magazines," explained the technician in charge of monitoring vital signs.

"Only to be expected."

Daniel nudged the professor. "Watch what happens in the next ten minutes."

Time ticked by. Gradually, four of the student's heart rates began to decrease. Bored, they put their magazines down and stared around the room with blank expressions. One of them picked up a copy of The Caravaner, studying the latest design in motor homes.

"Look!" exclaimed the professor. "Incredible!"

"You ain't seen nothing yet!"

The four students began to chat.

"Put their voices on speaker will you," ordered the professor. " I want to hear what they're saying."

One of the technicians flicked a switch, the students' voices filling the room.

"The match is on in a bit. FA Cup fourth round."

"Spurs verses Chelsea, yeah. Hope we get off in time to watch it."

"Did you see that documentary last night about Genghis Khan?"

"No. Spent the night with Sarah."

"Her with the huge tits from biochemistry?"

"Yeah.......Was it any good, the documentary?"

"Brilliant!"

"Shit! Sorry I missed it."

Daniel and the professor grinned at one another.

The technician pointed at the screen. "Look, Professor. The drug is having no effect on the gay student."

"I'm not surprised, if it doesn't work on women," said Daniel sarcastically.

"*Or* the student on the placebo! If anything his heart rate has increased!"

"OK, cue the pornography."

A hardcore porn video burst into life on a giant flat screen TV. It featured a busty Californian redhead and two black men. The action took place around swimming pool before moving into the bedroom. As the sex saga unfolded, the students on the chamcha paid little attention to the action, preferring instead the pages of Farmer's Weekly and Practical Model Railways, while the gay student and the placebo stared intently at the screen.

"Time to ramp up the tests," ordered the professor. "Ask the gay student to leave and send in the erotic dancers."

'Love To Love You Baby' by Donna Summer was piped into the room. Two voluptuous nineteen year olds wearing frilly black corsets with sequined trim entered slowly, arms entwined. Circling the group they pouted and blew kisses, pushing out their rouched bottoms provocatively, jiggling them and staring back at the students, tongues flicking like vipers. They began to dance, their beautiful bodies swaying like palm trees; hips, shoulders and thighs rippling in rhythmical seduction. Brazenly they undid each other's corsets, letting them fall to the floor......

"Heart rates?"

"Heart rates!" Professor Jameson glared at the technicians. All four were frozen to their seats ogling the dancers through the one-way glass. "For God's sake, concentrate! This is vital work we're doing here! It's not some peep show!"

"S.......sorry, Professor."

"Status?"

"Er......"

"Come on, man!"

"Pla.......placebo close dangerous pulse rate one eighty......er......."

"What the hell are you talking about!"

"I......I mean......I mean the professor's placebo....."

"Right! That's it! I've had enough! Get out! Go on, the lot of you! Out!"

Chamchad up, Daniel sat grinning as the technicians left the room, eyes flashing one last peep at the erotic dancers.

"Bloody outrageous!" spat the professor.

"Don't be too hard on them, they're only men after all."

An alarm buzzed on one of the consoles.

"What's that?" asked Daniel.

"The erection monitor. Each student has been fitted with specially designed underpants. As you can tell by the graph the student on the placebo is fully aroused."

"I don't need to look at the graph, Professor. Look, it sticks out a mile."

By now the dancers were naked and French kissing, kneading each other's breasts, sucking and caressing one another, lost in passionate intensity. The girls uncoupled and knelt down in front of the students. Ignoring the placebo with the hard on they concentrated instead on the three students whose indifferent expressions insulted their female pride, stroking their thighs and massaging their crotches.

"So Genghis Kahn, right, he attacks the Jin capital of Zhongdu. It's well defended obviously. But that doesn't stop him. His troops....."

"The Mongol hoards?"

"The Mongol hoards, yeah. They encircle Emperor Xuanzong's soldiers, slaughtering every last one of them and forcing him to move his capital south to Kaifeng."

"Wasn't he then Emperor who..........."

Professor Jameson's voice boomed over the speakers. "Thank you, ladies. You can stop now."

The dancers snatched up their corsets and left the room. The four students carried on talking, pointing out the various pros and cons of Khan's military campaign.

"Look at the student on the placebo!" exclaimed Daniel gleefully. "Look at his face!"

"Umm. He's completely shell-shocked."

"Poor shmuck."

Dazed, the professor shook his head. "I......I never thought it possible....What we've witnessed just now it's.....it's beyond comprehension. The amazing thing is, d'you see those two students there? The ones discussing Genghis Khan? Well, before the trial both had painful break ups with their long term girlfriends. Now look at them. They haven't got a care in the world. The potential for combating loneliness is enormous!"

"Yeah. Freedom'll fly off the shelves in bedsit land."

"My point entirely!.........All those lonely men, wanking themselves into a stupor night after night. Crying themselves to sleep for want of female companionship. You'll be their saviour. You might even get the Nobel Prize!"

"Hope so."

The professor's eyes blazed like comets as, Fuehrer like, he gazed off into a glorious thousand year Reich. "What you've discovered is nothing short of an 'anti female' vaccine. An antidote to all mankind's ills. I can see it now, global immunisation for all teenage boys. Millions growing up happy and contented. Because that's when it starts, you know; our obsession with the female form. One minute you're playing with your train set, the next your peeping into your sister's knicker draw. I suffered terribly during puberty. Humiliated I was. Made to feel like a pervert. All because I stole a kiss from the classroom sweetheart. The teacher, Miss Jenkins -- I can see her now, bloody Welsh dyke -- she dragged me out in front of the whole class and gave me the most awful dressing down, telling the girls to avoid me in the playground and to report me to the headmaster if I so much as looked at them! Can you imagine what that did to a sensitive mind? Can you!!?"

"Calm down, Professor."

"I was ostracised! Laughed at by all the girls! I tell you, if I could have laid my hands on a machinegun I'd have gone into that school and......"

"*Professor!*"

"I'm.....I'm terribly sorry."He poured out a glass of water and drank it down in one. "That's better. Got carried away there." The professor pressed a button on the console and spoke to the students through a microphone. "That concludes the trial. Thank you for your time."

"What happens now?" asked Daniel.

"I report the findings to JP Merrick. I'm sure he'll be thrilled."

* * *

"I'm thrilled, Daniel! Thrilled! I've studied the data and watched the video. I must say, those erotic dancers certainly got my pulse racing. How three red bloodied males could possibly ignore such rampant jezebels beggars belief. And look! The data proves it! Blood pressure normal, heart rate normal, and not a flicker from the erection monitor. It's a revelation!"

"Told you it would work."

"And did you *see* the girl's faces! They couldn't *believe* the students weren't interested in them."

"Yeah. Women hate being ignored."

"I mean, Genghis Khan! I ask you!"

They were sitting in JP's office overlooking the Thames. Daniel could see the City of London, its domes, spires and office blocks stretching away into the distant reaches of suburbia. Life was teeming all around him. The ordinary everyday life of men and women. All that was about to change. Once Freedom was on the market a new world order would be created, one that no longer used sex as a currency. He tried to imagine what sort of a world this would be; how women would possibly get by in such a society, but he couldn't. Instead his mind was filled with the billions he would earn from his discovery.

"I want to get Freedom into production as soon as possible," said JP impatiently, mindful of the domestic pogrom Barbara was carrying out at Oldthorpe. Determined to extract revenge for his outrageous behaviour, she was making his life a living hell. Again and again she grilled him as to why he had acted the way he did. He told her he didn't know, that it was just one of those things, similar to when -- one time in a thousand -- a fox suddenly turns on the hounds.

"So I'm a *dog* now, am I! Well let me tell you something! This one's got sharp teeth! And she's *not* afraid to use them! And while we're on the subject, a little bird in the Post Office told me you attended a hunt meeting at the pub. Is that correct?"

"What night's this?"

"Don't take me for a fool, JP! The night you came home and started throwing your weight around!"

"Well I er......I just happen to wander in, yes."

"Oh! you just happened to 'wander in', did you? Well you can forget all about hunting! Those days are over! Just what is it with you men anyway, always wanting to chase things? From now on this estate is a hunting free zone! Starting with that ridiculous gun room of yours. I want the whole lot cleared out and sold! Do you understand?"

"But Barbara, those guns have been in the family for generations. They're Edmond's birthright!"

"You should have thought about that before you turned on me! I'll never forgive you for speaking to me like that! Never!"

Daniel lifted his briefcase and placed it on JP'S desk, snapping open the lid.

Inside was a large plastic bag packed with chamcha roots.

JP gazed at them, mesmerised. He reached out and ran his hand over the bag's knobbly surface, sighing, wistfully, "Freedom."

"How, er.....how did you get on, you know, the day you took it?"

JP's eyes glazed over. "I can only describe the experience as 'total liberation.' A bit like when the French finally got rid of the Nazis."

"That good, eh?"

"Oh it was marvellous. It's hard to put into words the sheer ecstasy." His voice trailed into a whisper. "I want to feel like that forever."

Daniel knew the answer to the question, but asked anyway. "How are things at home......at the moment?"

JP winced. "Vile. My wife wants her pound of flesh. Every last ounce of it. Vindictive cow." He stamped his foot in frustration. "Oh why can't I stand up for myself for pity's sake! I mean *look* at me. I'm a powerful man! I run a multinational company! And it's not just me. Most of the board are in the same boat. Take Ping Yan Lou. Before he joined Global Pharmaceuticals he was head of the secret police -- a brutal and repressive organisation feared throughout China -- yet that man can't sneeze without his wife's say so. And look at *Signor* Fabretti! A colossus in the world of finance, but do you know, I've actually seen him cower at the mere mention of his wife's name. No wonder Hitler shot himself the moment he got married. He knew what was coming. Yes, say what you like about the Fuehrer, at least he had foresight." He slammed his fist down onto the desk. "Why are men so bloody subservient!!? They're only woman after all!"

Daniel saw his father collapsing onto the hall carpet in tears. "The sooner the contract's sorted the better."

"Oh yes, the contract! Our legal department is drawing it up as we speak. Should be ready by the end of next week.....As for the money......" JP scribbled the amount on a piece of paper and handed it to Daniel. "I'm sure you'll agree, Global Pharmaceuticals have been extremely generous."

Now it was Daniel's turn to be mesmerised. He stared transfixed at the amount. It was like one of those crazy equations boffins come up with to describe the odds of a meteor hitting the Earth. "Wow.....I.......I don't know what to say......It's more money than I've ever dreamed."

"You deserve it, Daniel. Really. In my book you're up there with Sir Alexander Fleming. More so. Fleming only got rid of a few microbes."

"What now?"

"Once you've signed the contract the roots will be taken to our laboratory in Suffolk to be synthesised and made into tablets. In the meantime our marketing department swings into action. The plan is to leak the drug gradually to the media........Sort of slow release."

"I can't wait, Mr Merrick."

"Nor can I.......And please, call me JP."

CHAPTER TWELVE

"This afternoon, Mr Page? What time?"

"Three o'clock suit you?"

"Three's fine. See you later then."

Nick ended the call. Why the hell had Charles Page rang him on a Saturday to invite him over to his house? Perhaps he was selling the company and wanted to let him know before making an official announcement? He was that type of boss -- kind and considerate, especially to his long term employees. Charles hadn't been himself since Daniel skedaddled off to London. The joy had gone out of him. At a meeting two days ago he barely spoke, shuffling his papers and staring at Daniel's empty seat. He'd obviously had enough. Which was a shame because, despite the disastrous trip to the Amazon, profits were up and a brand new research facility was only weeks away from opening.

So instead of trawling through internet dating sites like he usually did on a Saturday, Nick decided to drive into Wilmslow town centre. A good strong coffee was called for while he pondered his future. And he knew just the place -- an independent coffee shop called Rise. One of his neighbours went there, a fifty year old Irish firecracker whose relationship with her partner had run aground more often than a tanker off the Cornish coast. Apparently he was a miserable sod who took her for granted. Walking down Kings Road past their house the other night Nick heard her screaming, "That's it, Paul! I've had enough! I'm putting the house on the market!" Another relationship down the pan. But judging by her short sparkly dresses and penchant for glitzy wine bars it wouldn't be long before *she* was back on the market.

Nick took a quick shower. He changed into beige coloured chinos and an open neck blue shirt, splashing on a extra dose of Paco Rabanne. Walking into Rise he spotted the firecracker in the corner stirring her coffee.

Poor woman, she looked so miserable. He thought about going over but thought better of it. According to his next door neighbour Steve -- the macho fireman -- she was one of those needy types who uses men to get what she wants, casting aside friends when surplus to requirements. Maybe Steve was right. Maybe she was a shallow, manipulative cow. Or maybe she just wanted to be loved. Nick ordered a coffee and found a seat opposite. He tried to catch her eye but she was busy on her mobile. Those dating Apps. Like one arm bandits. You never know what you're going to pull.

"Nick, isn't it?"

He looked up. A gorgeous blonde girl was smiling at him. She looked familiar.

"Sophie........Daniel's ex........We met at the company bash two months ago."

"Oh God, yeah! Sophie! I didn't recognise you. Have you changed your hair?"

"Thought I'd go short." She touched her fringe nervously. "Not sure if it suits me."

"Oh it *does*! Makes you like a young Mia Farrow!"

"Thanks....Can I join you?"

"Sure! Sit down! How are you?"

"Can't complain. You?"

"Not bad. Would you like a coffee?"

"Just ordered one, thanks. Can I ask you about Daniel. There's a lot of rumours flying around. I mean, you were in the rainforest with him? What happened? I hear you both got into a fight over a gorge."

The rumours, started by himself and exaggerated daily in the staff canteen, had now reached disaster movie proportions. A crocodile had somehow got involved, snapping at their feet as they fought on a rickety rope bridge seconds away from snapping.

She huddled up close, staring right at him, her crystalline green eyes like atolls seen from space. God she was beautiful. Nick puffed out his chest. "Well, we'd been trekking for just over a week. One day we came to a part of the forest destroyed by loggers. It was our search area you see, and there was nothing left but burnt grass and charred stumps of wood. I was absolutely devastated. Anyway Daniel stared to laugh, saying he didn't give a shit about the rainforest and how they could concrete it over as far as he was concerned. So I hit him."

"Good for you. I hear he came at you with a knife, and tried to push you off a cliff."

"That as well."

She found his modesty refreshing, so different from the usual macho bullshit spouted by Wilmslow Alpha males. "Imagine saying that about the rainforest. I was always taught at school how important it is to the world. I'd love to go."

"Would you!"

"It's on my bucket list......Is it as beautiful as everyone makes out?"

"Oh yeah!.......Mind you, Daniel didn't think so. He was more interested in the girls in Rio."

"Really?"

"First night we were there I caught him sneaking one back to his room."

"And all the time he was texting me, telling me how much he loved me! *God,* you think you know someone......Mind you, Daniel always was sex mad."

"You don't miss him, then?"

His question bordered on the intrusive, but she was glad to unburden herself. "To be honest, Nick, I don't know what I ever saw in him."

"I know what you mean. Arrogant sod."

"Is it true he's living on the streets?"

"Who told you that! No, one of Charles' friends saw him in the bar at the Dorchester. Apparently he's got a suite there."

"The Dorchester! Bloody hell! I phoned him the other day and offered to send him some money! What an idiot! And d'you know what he said?" She lowered her voice. "He told me to go fuck myself."

"Typical Daniel." That was nice, the way she said 'fuck' just then, right into his ear.

She took a sip of coffee. "What I can't understand is, why he's burnt all his bridges. I mean, how's he going to earn a living? The way he spends money he'll be broke within a year."

"Search me."

"It's his dad I feel sorry for. I saw him last week. Poor man, he looked awful."

"I know. He's invited me over to his house. Between you and me I think he might be selling the company. Don't say anything."

"Course not." She sighed. "Daniel had the world on a plate, and he's managed to mess things up........If Charles *does* sell the company, will you stay on?"

"Probably not. Time for a change. I'm fed up of Wilmslow."

"I know what you mean. Shallow place."

Nick tried his hand at humour. "More culture in Australia."

Sophie burst out laughing. "Definitely!"

Leave! Leave on a high! Nick finished his coffee and stood up. He glanced at his watch. "Must be going. Charles is expecting me." A look of disappointment flashed across her face. *YES!* "Nice chatting with you, Sophie. You take care now."

"And you. See you around, yeah."

On his way out he paid the bill. "Send one of those nice cakes over to that blonde girl there. And get her another coffee." He gave the waiter a tenner. "That should cover it."

He drove to Alderley Edge on a high. The world looked so different to when he first woke up this morning. Brighter. Crisper. Thank God he hadn't stayed in and trawled the internet! Soul destroying. What did she say? "See you around, yeah." Wow. And fancy her wanting to go to the rainforest!

He'd been to his boss's house before -- two years ago for a company barbecue thrown for senior staff. It was held in the Page's vast back garden overlooking Alderley Edge golf course. All afternoon Daniel had lorded it over the griddle, dressed in one of those stupid French Maid aprons, the ones with the false breasts. The next morning Nick suffered terrible food poisoning. To this day he was convinced Daniel had purposely given him an underdone pork sausage.

It was a lovely house, so different from the bland semi he was brought up in. Another world, as his mother used to say. At least he'd work hard to get where he was and not relied on some doting father. If only! He tapped politely on the front door.

"Ah, Nick! Glad you could make it! Come in, come in." They crossed the hall and walked into the lounge. "Take a seat. Tea?"

"No thanks, Mr Page."

"Charles, please!"

A first! Nick cast his eye around the room -- high stuccoed ceiling, deep shag pile carpet, expensive furnishings. He imagined Daniel tearing round as a child. He glanced at the luxurious sofa, thinking of the first time Sophie must have sat there, a lamb to the slaughter.

Charles sat down on a red leather armchair studded with brass buttons. "You're probably wondering why I asked you here?"

"Yes, Mr......Charles! I am a bit intrigued."

"Well, I've been doing a lot of thinking recently........"

Here we go, thought Nick.

"......and I've decided, in light of my son's obnoxious behaviour......."

To sell the company.

"..........to restructure the company."

"Really?"

"You sound surprised, Nick."

"To be honest I thought you were about to retire."

"Good God, no! Not until the company's on a secure footing. I *had* hoped to hand things over to Daniel, but deep down I knew that was never an option. The boy takes after his mother I'm afraid -- headstrong and more than a little greedy. So what I intend to do Nick, is......"

Make you redundant.

"..............promote you onto the board."

"What!!?"

"Don't be so modest. I value your passion and integrity. You sum up all that's best about Page Pharmaceuticals." He leaned forward in his chair. "I want to make you Head of Research. You'll have a whole department to yourself, not to mention a brand new research facility. I'm giving you carte blanche to pursue a whole range of illnesses, from Alzheimer's to the Zika virus. What's more, as from today I'm doubling your salary."

"Bloody hell!....S....sorry, Mr.....*Charles!*"

"Is that a yes?"

"Absolutely it's a yes!"

"Excellent! This calls for a glass of bubbly! Shan't be a moment."

When Charles disappeared into the wine cellar Nick had a quick look round. He noticed a photograph of a young woman on the mantelpiece. He walked over and picked it up, examining it closely. She was absolutely stunning -- a cut glass figurine exquisitely coutured in Chanel. Daniel's mother, obviously. She was well bred to the point of madness. Her eyes, skittish and electrifying, were designed to see into men's souls, to discover their weaknesses and ruthlessly exploit them. Kind-hearted and benevolent when pleased; malicious and vengeful when not. There was no such thing as not getting her own way. Her beauty would not allow it. So this was the woman who had almost bankrupted Charles both emotionally and financially. Rumours swirled for years about her wild behaviour -- her ferocious spending sprees, her gothic mood swings, her thousand and one lovers -- carried out for the sole purpose of humiliating him. It was said she liked nothing better than to flirt with some handsome man in Charles' presence, leaving him heartbroken. Time and time again her forgave her, until, contemptuous of his puppy dog eyes and priest like devotion, she ran off with an Argentinean polo player. Nick stared at the photograph. What man wouldn't ruin himself over a woman like that.

"At last!" Charles came back into the room clutching a dusty bottle of vintage Krug and two champagne flutes. "I *had* hoped to open this when Daniel took over the firm. Won't be happening now." Poor Charles, he'd lost the two people in the world most dear to him. Love hurts. He popped the cork and filled both glasses. "Well, cheers Nick! Here's to Page Pharmaceuticals!"

CHAPTER THIRTEEN

REPORTER FOUND DEAD IN SUFFOLK BEAUTY SPOT

MYSTERY BAFFLES POLICE

The body of freelance journalist Ann Crowther was discovered last night in remote woodland close to the village of Amblethorpe. Police say she'd been strangled.

Miss Crowther, who wrote for the *Guardian* newspaper on feminist issues, was found by a local man out walking his dog. Mr Pat Collins, a forty year old cleaner from the nearby Global Pharmaceuticals research facility, said he found the body under three feet of earth. 'If my dog hadn't started digging she'd never have been found.'

Friends of Miss Crowther say she'd gone to Amblethorpe following a tipoff from an anonymous source.

The lift doors opened onto the penthouse suit. The estate agent, a smartly dressed man in his forties with impeccable manners, handed Daniel a glossy brochure. "If you'd care to step this way, Mr Page."

He was led through a series of luxuriously furnished rooms specially designed for the billionaire about town. Stuffed with every possible gadget, it was a wonderland of sleek surfaces and ultra modern decor.

"The penthouse comes fully furnished."

"Good. Life's too short to go picking out sofas."

"Master bedroom, en-suite bathroom."

"Very nice."

"All the fixtures and fittings -- taps, plugs, light switches etc -- are gold plated. His and Hers sinks, as you can see. Oh yes, and the Jacuzzi is fashioned from the finest Carrara marble."

"I wouldn't expect anything less."

"Now let me show you the kitchen."

"Bloody hell, its massive!"

"Designed and fitted by Clive Christian, naturally."

"Naturally."

"If sir would like to step out onto the roof garden."

"Oh wow! What a view!"

"One of the finest in London, Mr Page."

"Look! You can see right into the House of Parliament! Amazing!"

"Glad you like it."

"Right, let's cut to the chase."

"As you wish. The penthouse is on the market for six point eight million."

"I'll take it."

Daniel jumped into a taxi and headed for the City. He was on his way to Global Pharmaceuticals to sign the contract. For the past week he'd taken part in his own unique experiment he called 'Best of Both Worlds.' Using himself as a guinea pig he stopped taking his daily dose of chamcha and waited to see what would happen. Alone in his suite at the Dorchester he noted the various stages of withdrawal. For the first few hours nothing. Then a gradual awareness of feminine shapes -- the voluptuous curve of a bedside lamp, the sensual sweep of an art nouveau mirror, the sudden appreciation of a bowl of fresh peaches. He jotted down 'mouth dry' 'pulse rate increasing.' Then a knock at the door and the real thing. He hadn't noticed her before -- the gorgeous Lithuanian maid -- though she'd brought coffee to his room several times; eyes flashing, always giving him the come on; until finally she'd given up, convinced he was gay.

"Hi."

"*Hkkkk*ello."

As she leaned over and put the coffee down on a side table, he noted 'losing control' 'lustful thoughts returning'. When she'd gone he paced the room, jotting in his notebook 'hitting the town tonight' 'deffo' 'sex on my terms' 'fucking awesome!'

Freed from the effects of the drug Mother Nature wrenched back control. After dining in the hotel restaurant he strolled over to an exclusive Mayfair club, drowning himself in alcohol and cocaine, five, six, seven girls in his VIP booth. He chose two and took them back to his suite, kicking them out once the threesome was over. The second they closed the door a feeling of emptiness swept over him. Finding himself alone he thought about Sophie, how much he loved her. Distraught, he dived into the bathroom and stuffed a root of chamcha in his mouth. Ten minutes later he was as calm as a Hindu cow. Wondering what all the fuss was about he went to bed and slept like a baby.

The cab pulled up outside Global Pharmaceuticals head office. "Fifteen quid, mate."

Daniel gave the driver a crisp twenty. "Keep the change." He got out and strolled into reception. "I'm here for a meeting with JP Merrick."

"Oh yes, Mr Page. He's expecting you. Do got up."

He got into the lift and was whisked to the thirtieth floor. When the doors opened JP was there to greet him. He looked stressed.

"Is everything alright?" asked Daniel. "You still want me to sign the contract?"

"Of course, dear boy! But not today." JP ushered him into his office and closed the door. "We've run into a slight problem."

"Problem?"

"Don't worry, I'm sure it'll be rectified. It's our lab; they're having trouble extracting the drug from the roots. I'm afraid the potency's degenerated. We need to get hold of some fresh samples and freeze-dry them on the spot. I'm sending two of our chemists into the rainforest. I'd be most grateful if you could let me have the exact location of the tribe."

Daniel's suspicious nature kicked in. "I better go with them! It's the tribe, you see. They're suspicious of strangers. If your chemists turn up unannounced they'll get butchered."

"Good God!......Well, if you don't mind?"

"Not at all. Plus I know a guide who can lead us straight to them."

"Very well. They're flying out first thing in the morning on one of our corporate jets. I'll send a car to the Dorchester at 6am to pick you up."

"Great." Oh no, thought Daniel. I've got to go back to that shit hole!

* * *

Surrounded by laboratory paraphernalia Nick was peering into an electron microscope. The new enzyme he was studying seemed to have miraculous properties that.........

"Nick! Telephone."

"Who is it?"

"She didn't say."

She? He got up and walked towards the wall-mounted phone. He was about to pick up the receiver when he noticed Ben hanging around in earshot. "Take that Petri dish over to Giles in biotech." He waited until Ben had left the room. "Hello. Nick Slater."

"Hi, Nick. It's Sophie."

Sophie?..........*SOPHIE!* "Oh hi, Sophie. What can I do for you?"

"Just wondered if you fancy going for a drink tonight?"

"I've not heard anything more about Daniel, if that's what you want to know."

"God, no! It's not that!"

His heart started pounding. "Well..........well what is it then?"

"Just thought it'd be nice to hook up, that's all. I enjoyed our chat the other day. I mean, if you'd rather not......."

"No! No! I'd *love* to!.....W....where? W....what time? Should I pick you up?"

"That's alright. I'll meet you in the Coach and Four at eight."

"Great! Look forward to it, Sophie."

"Me too. Bye."

"Bye....Bye." He put the phone down. *BLOODY HELL!!!!!!! SOPHIE!!!*.......Calm down. She's lonely. She wants someone to talk to. Why me? Her friends are probably busy. Typical!.......Fuck it I'm going!

For the rest of the afternoon he found it impossible to concentrate. The miraculous enzyme he'd been studying -- the one that promised a breakthrough in all sorts of areas -- no longer interested him. In fact he couldn't give a damn if it cured every known aliment on the planet. Something inside him told him this was more than just an innocent drink. He'd detected in her voice a warmth rare as summer snow. The last time a woman had spoken to him like that was...........well, never.

"Who was that?" asked Ben, intrigued by the sudden change in Nick's demeanour. He no longer had a scowl on his face. He was gazing out of the window like a lovesick teenager.

"Never you mind.....Darr da dee dar dar."

Five o'clock and he was out the door. Straight home and straight into the shower. A full hour to get ready. Another two to kill. He tried to eat but couldn't. Constant glancing in the mirror. Too smart? Too casual? That'll do. Smart casual. Stop it now. Calm down. That lovely hotel in Keswick. Sophie would love it there. Get a grip! Probably never see her again after tonight.

7:50. Time to go! Nice evening. Think I'll stroll into town. Wilmslow looks nice. Couples dinning alfresco. Very South of France. Here we go. Walk in and stroll to the bar. There she is there she is! Bloody hell she looks gorgeous........God she's smiling!

"Hi, Nick!"

"Hi!"

* * *

The sleeker than a bullet Gulfstream touched down at Manaus International Airport. Daniel remembered the last time he was here; how Nick had droned on throughout the flight about the importance of the rainforest. Turns out he was right. Who'd have thought it. That drongo.

The steward pushed open the door. A blast of humid air filled the cabin. Daniel grabbed his bag and filed down the aircraft steps, followed by the two chemists. He'd got to know them during the flight. Tim and Paul. Nice guys. They were in awe of him, talking nonstop about the benefits of Freedom. How it would 'change the world.' Tim admitted he had a jealous streak when it came to women, and longed for the day he could trust his wife. Paul's problem was that no matter how much sex he had he always wanted more.

A limo purring on the tarmac took them to the five star Tropical Hotel in downtown Manaus. After checking in Daniel rang Ortega Tours, the same company they used on their last trip. He spoke to the boss, requesting Pacon as his guide. The boss confirmed he was available and said he would meet them tomorrow morning. So far so good. He wandered down into the lobby and bought a copy of the *Herald Tribune.* Relaxing in the bar he came across a striking double page ad containing one word -- **FREEDOM** -- emblazoned across both pages.

The next morning, after an early breakfast, the limo sped across town, dropping them outside Ortega's head office. There was Pacon, God bless him, sitting in his

Land Rover with the door open; the same cowboy boots, the same cynical expression, a cigarette wedged between his lips. They greeted each other like old friends.

"I did not think you would be back so soon!" exclaimed Pacon.

Daniel laughed. "Neither did I! How's your wife?"

"Sweet as ever."

The fresh bruise on the side of his face said otherwise. Daniel put his arm around Pacon's shoulder. "I want you to take us to the Atori village again. I know, I know, I'm a sucker for giant rat. Seriously, we need to do more research."

"It will be my pleasure. I've not been back to their village since you and your compardres last visit."

"The tribe are still there aren't they?"

"Oh yes. A fisherman I know saw them only last week. The river near their village is very bountifu....."

"What about Kinta? Is he still with the tribe -- only I got on really well with him last time."

"Ah yes, Kinta! I heard you and he developed quite a friendship. What that man doesn't know about plants isn't worth........"

"Is he there or not!!?"

Western impatience always amused Pacon. What was the rush for heaven's sake. "Yes, yes, he's still there."

"Brilliant.....Right, let's go."

It was Tim and Paul's first field trip to the Amazon rainforest so the ten hour drive proved fascinating -- the flora and fauna, the sheer immensity of it all.

Daniel noticed their wide-eyed innocence, and decided to give them a treat. He nudged Pacon. "Hey. How about taking us to that bar tonight; the one on the waterfront. I want my friends to see that mind blowing barmaid. You know, the one we saw last time."

"We can go to the bar, sir, but I'm afraid she no longer works there."

"Since when?"

"Not long after your visit an American film company arrived to shoot a Hollywood blockbuster. One night I took the director -- a very famous man, I forget his name -- to the bar for a drink. Well, the moment he set eyes on her he became obsessed. After filming was over he took her back to Los Angeles and married her. Who can blame him." He kissed the tips of his fingers. "What a gem!"

Oh no, thought Daniel. It's started. The destruction of mankind. Like a dangerous virus escaping from a government laboratory she had found her way to the epicentre of decadence. There she would flourish, wreaking havoc on the male sex. Daniel saw the whole thing. First she would have an affair with a leading actor, beguiling him with her sensuality. Her husband would find out and kill himself, leaving her all his money. She would move on from actors to producers, seducing them into giving her the lead in one of their films. Soon the whole world would get to appreciate her beauty. A billionaire and front runner for the Presidency would next be ensnared, marrying her after storming to victory in the primaries. With her on his arm he was a shoe-in. Ensconced in the White House as First Lady, she would charm presidents and prime ministers, a steamy affair with a British royal prince inevitable. Then, following a fling with a Mafia boss, the President and Vice President would be assassinated in a series of mysterious shootings. The entire country would be thrown into turmoil. ISIS and Al-Qaeda blamed. A motherly hand on the tiller would be called for. And then she would step forward. The obvious choice. With her diamond encrusted finger on the nuclear button it was only a matter of time before something displeased her, triggering World War Three.

"Is everything alright, sir?" asked Pacon, noticing Daniel's sweat-drench forehead and mad staring eyes.

"Yeah, yeah. I'm OK. Bit hot in here, that's all." He wiped his brow and thought, I need to find that fucking plant, and fast!

The Land Rover arrived in Pacon's village just as the sun was going down. Little had changed since his last visit. The river still flowed beneath the line of broken down shacks; raggedy children ran riot amongst upturned fishing boats; and there, towering above everything -- a brooding presence -- the dark green mass of the rainforest.

While Tim and Paul unloaded the special container brought along to freeze-dry the chamcha roots, Daniel noticed Pacon blowing kisses to his wife. She was standing outside their shack, arms folded, a stern expression on her face. "Hey, Pacon! Are we staying at your place tonight?"

"Er...no...I have er....I have found you alternative accommodation with a cousin of mine. His wife is away visiting a sick relative, so he has agreed to put you up. I hope it won't be too inconvenient?"

"Whatever."

"I must warn you.....His er....his house is a little foul smelling, owing to its proximity to the sewer."

"Charming."

Pacon wasn't wrong. The fetid hovel not only stank it was infested with flees and cockroaches. Only a bottle of sugarcane rum got them off to sleep, Daniel's ironic "Welcome to the jungle!" the last thing Tim and Paul heard before they crashed onto the raffia matting.

The next morning, after a disgusting breakfast of cold rice and black beans, they set off up river in Pacon's canoe.

"Not a patch on your place," said Daniel.

Pacon steered the canoe to the very centre of the river. "Thank you, sir. My cousin's wife, she is bone idle. That is what happens when you marry a domineering woman."

169

Daniel smirked, dripping sarcasm. " Not like you, eh, Pacon?"

From the back of the canoe came a dreadful silence, followed by a nervous clearing of the throat.

For the next few hours the rainforest glided past like stage scenery. Daniel kept delving into his rucksack, making sure Kinta's gift was still there -- a fabulous bejewelled knife he'd picked up in a curio shop in Manaus. A foot long and sharp as a razor, its stainless steel blade was carved with wave like patterns and leaping fish. One look at it and Kinta would be pliant as plastercine.

"Not far now," announced Pacon, steering the canoe expertly past a floating log that from a distance resembled a giant crocodile.

Daniel dug his paddle into the water, increasing the speed of the canoe. He couldn't wait to get there, find the plants and get the hell out. Up ahead he recognised a distinctive tree Pacon had pointed out last time. And rounding the bend there was the sliver of sandy beach where, Cook like, they'd first set foot ashore. "We're here! We're here!"

Pacon breached the canoe onto the sand.

Daniel jumped out. "Where are they?"

"Have patience," said Pacon, exasperated. "First I must call to let them know we are here."

"Oh yeah. That bird sound you made.....Well, go on then!"

They definitely weren't paying him enough! Pacon cupped his hands to his mouth and sent forth a plangent, bird like call.

"Where are they!!?"

"Sir, please, give them a little time. There are no motorcars in the rainforest."

Fifteen minutes dragged by. Daniel pounded up and down the sand. "They know we're coming, right?"

"Yes, sir. I sent word only yesterday."

"Good. Because....."

"Ah!"

"Are they here?"

"No, sir. But they are expecting us. See! There, above the trees, a kilometre away, where their village is? Smoke is rising. They are obviously preparing a feast of welcome."

"What are we waiting for? Let's go!"

Pacon unsheathed his machete and led them into the dense undergrowth, hacking through braches and low hanging vines. After an hour's slog Daniel could smell meat cooking on an open fire. "I'm starving!"

"Just through here, sir." They came to a clearing. Pacon dropped his machete. "Oh sweet Mary!"

An area the size of Bristol yawned in front of them, blackened, charred and burning. All that was left of the Atori village was a few smouldering stumps. Bodies littered the ground; men, women and children lying in scattered ranks, shot through with bullet holes.

"*NO!!!!!*" Daniel ran towards the carnage.

Pacon chased after him. "Sir! Be careful! The loggers might still be here!"

He took out the knife meant for Kinta, waving it around and yelling. "Good! I'll kill the bastards!"

Sir, sir. There is nothing you can do. We must go quickly."

"Not until I've found what I'm looking for!" He went from body to body, rolling them over and scanning their faces. "Kinta? Kinta?"

A groan came from a nearby group of huddled together corpses. It was Kinta, barely alive, his chest riddled with bullet wounds. Daniel ran over and knelt down beside him. "Look, Kinta! I've brought you a knife! Look! Nice, isn't it?"

Kinta coughed up a gourde of blood. "Cham.....chamcha."

"That's right, Kinta! You remembered! Chamcha! Where is it?"

"Sir, he is dying!"

"Shut up! ....Go on, Kinta. What did you say? Chamcha. Just point to it."

Softly came his final word, "*Cham.....cha.*"

"Kinta! *NO!!!*"

Pacon placed a comforting hand on Daniel's shoulder. "Sir. It is no use. He is dead."

Daniel stood up. "We'll have to find another tribe!"

"Another tribe?"

"I need to collect samples!"

"Then your trip has been in vain. The Atori were the last to hold the secret knowledge of the rainforest. That is why I brought you here." His eyes scoured the parched horizon. "Now everything is lost."

Daniel seized Pacon by the shoulders. "*No!* What I'm looking for *must* be close by! Kinta tried to tell me before he died. You *heard* him!"

"But, sir......Kinta was calling for his mother."

"W....what?"

"Chamcha..... it's the Atori word for mother."

"Bollocks! It's the name of the plant I'm looking for!"

"Then it must have been very special to them. The Atori named only their most sacred things 'Mother'.

Daniel's mouth gaped open. "M....mother?" He sank to his knees, crashing full length onto the ground. It felt warm and comforting beneath his cheek. Digging his nails into the rich black soil he stared out across the desolate plain. He closed his eyes and hugged the earth, whispering.........."*Mother.*"

16637202R00104

Printed in Great Britain
by Amazon